THE GUILDSMAN

A Vow of Succour

By Ryan Darkfield

Acknowledgements

Roger Victor Richards
Glyn, Claire and Lucas Richards
Sarah Baugh
Chris and Donna Edwards
Warren McCabe
Ash Fowkes
Clement Baugh
Chase

and
Gaynor Richards

Map Of Ethren

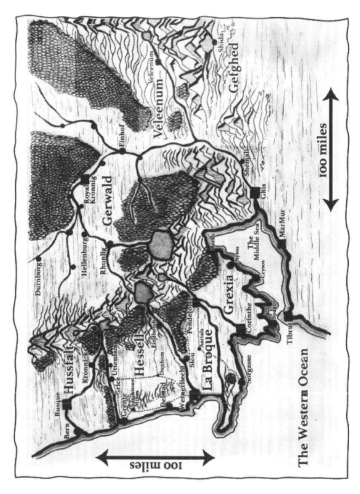

Prologue

Something shrieked in the courtyard.

The sound woke Kurgen Mollat with a start.

He groaned and sat up in his bed.

He rubbed his sore shoulders, cursing his age and infirmity.

Time had treated him cruelly.

Then again, so had everything else.

He pulled away the sheets and lifted his scrawny legs out of the cot, dropping his feet down onto the cold uncarpeted floor.

He shivered.

The year had not yet turned, but the air was cool.

He dreaded the onset of Winter.

Would he survive another one?

He had to.

His plan to be the richest man in Gerwald depended on it.

He planted his hands on the sides of the bed and lifted himself to his feet.

The room was dark, the only light coming from the glow of the Harvest Moon, which shone through a break in the curtains.

He made his way over to the window and pulled apart the blinds.

His reflection stared back at him in the glass.

The face he saw was creased and worn, covered in blotches and liver spots.

He sighed then rued the passing of his long-lost youth.

His breath steamed up the glass.

He wipcd it away then gazed out into the yard.

There was nothing there.

For a moment, he wondered whether or not the sound he'd heard had been a dream, but then, out of the corner of his eye, he saw a small black shape darting across the court.

It was a cat, a stray from Durnborg.

It stopped at the wall then leapt up it in a single bound before it scurried away into the field towards the lights of the town.

What I'd give to be able to run like that, he thought to himself, as he shut the curtains and made his way back to the bed.

As he lifted up the sheets, he was startled by a noise that came from downstairs.

It was a creaking sound, like a door that had been ajar.

Had someonc broken in?

The thought of it made him more angry than scared.

He'd spent his life amassing his fortune and was not going to let some ruffian invade his home and take it from him.

Still, if a challenge was to be made, it was sensible to do so armed.

He glanced towards the fireplace.

Resting on the hearth was an iron poker.

He walked over then leant down to pick it up.

5

At once he yelled and the thing fell from his hands, clattering down onto the wooden floorboards below.

For a second, he'd forgotten about his condition.

Last summer, he'd been stricken with apoplexy, an illness that had deprived him of the use of his right hand. Being as stalwart as he was, he'd not let the affliction get the better of him and had learned to get by regardless. For the most part, he'd managed well, but there were still a few things he struggled with, like tying his shoes, writing letters...

Or wielding pokers.

Cursing under his breath, he bent down and picked up the metal rod with his left hand.

He then rose to his feet and made his way to the door.

Holding it ajar, he peered outside.

The hallway was empty.

He stepped out onto the landing and made his way forward to the balustrade, where he leant over the rail and looked down upon the entrance hall.

Boxes brimming with baubles, ornaments and trinkets were stacked up around the walls.

They were the obvious target for any would-be thief, but it seemed as if none had been opened or molested.

So, what had made the sound?

He crept along the landing to the staircase

then quietly descended to the ground floor.

At the bottom, he stopped and listened.

He heard nothing but the sound of the wind whistling through the hedgerows outside.

He went over to the boxes for a closer look, then felt the touch of a cool breeze on his cheek.

He stopped dead in his tracks.

Somewhere in the house, a door or window was open.

Maybe there was an intruder after all...?

He turned his face in the direction of the breeze.

It was coming from the Study.

The door of the room was ajar, moving on its hinges in time with the gusts blowing outside.

He took a breath to steel himself, then made his way toward it.

"If anyone's in there," he said, "You'd better come out and show yourself."

No one answered.

He stepped up to the doorframe and peeked inside.

The room was cluttered with boxes, papers, and an assortment of bric-a-brac that he'd collected over the years. Most of it was stacked up around the large chestnut desk.

Behind it was a large window.

Like the fenestra upstairs, the glass panes were hidden from view by a set of long curtains.

He stepped inside the room.

It was cold, and the chilly air tickled the exposed skin of his legs and ankles.

The curtains moved.

He took another breath then paced forward, moving as quietly as possible.

He lifted up the poker.

Using its tip, he slowly parted the curtains.

The window was open.

A cold gust blew outside.

The blinds shivered. The papers littering the desk flapped, and his father's rocking chair, which sat in the corner, creaked on its bows.

Was that the sound he'd heard?

Another gust blew.

This one was stronger than the last.

The old seat quivered back and forth, and its curved wooden legs squeaked as they rubbed against the oaken floor.

Mollat sighed.

The mystery was solved.

Or was it?

He stared at the open window.

Unless his memory was playing tricks on him, he was sure he'd closed it before bed...

It was part of his nightly routine.

It was a methodical process.

It had to be.

His house was large, with many doors and windows.

The process took time.

But it was worth it to avoid being murdered in his sleep...

That had always been his greatest fear, and he shuddered at the thought of it.

He looked at the window and wondered if someone may have jimmied it open.

No, he thought. *To do so they would have needed to break the glass...*

More likely, he'd simply forgotten to shut it.

But if that was the case, why was he so convinced he had?

He'd once heard a physician say that the mind was always the last thing to go.

Maybe this was the beginning of the end for him?

He shook his head and cursed his decrepit body.

If he were younger, he wouldn't have been so careless...

He remembered how strong he'd been back then.

He'd fought in the War of the Ascension, serving as a Pikeman in the Imperial Army. He'd been lean and tall and muscular. His comrades used to call him 'the Ox'. Whenever a task required brute force, they'd call on him to help.

"Fetch the Ox," they used to say. "He'll do it...."

But those days were long gone.

And life and time were cruel companions.

He placed the poker down on the desk then pulled the window shut, fixing the latch tightly against the frame.

At once, the room quietened.

The chair stopped rocking and the papers came to rest in their stacks.

He picked up the poker, then left the room and started making his way back up the staircase.

As he turned onto the landing, he suddenly froze.

Up ahead, a shadowy figure stood halfway along the passage. It was hiding amongst the boxes that had been stacked against the walls.

"Who's that?" Mollat called.

The shadow didn't answer.

"Get out of my house," he yelled.

The figure didn't budge.

Kurgen lifted up the tip of his poker.

Leave now and I swear I won't harm you," he growled.

There was no response.

Mollat was gripped with rage.

"Fine," he barked. "If that's the way you want it."

He came forward and raised the poker high above his head. With an angry wipe he brought it down squarely upon the figure's head. The blow brought the man down, and he fell to the floor at his feet.

Mollat looked down at the body, and at once he realised it wasn't a man at all, but a mannequin, used for mummer's shows, which had been stored amongst the boxes.

The strike from the poker had damaged its head and the straw stuffing within had spilt out over the floorboards.

Kurgen tutted to himself.

He'd remembered buying the piece from a troubadour, in the winter of ninety-seven. The man had told him it was worth one hundred Drams, but Mollat had haggled him down to fifty.

It had been a good investment.

But now it was worthless.

He placed the poker against the rail of the balustrade and reached down to pick it up.

Maybe he could mend it with a needle and thread?

No, he thought. *It was a job that needed two hands.*

He cursed his misfortune.

Maybe Eva would fix it for him?

She was his seamstress, and as luck would have it, she was coming tomorrow.

Perhaps he could convince her to give him a discount?

He would be a returning customer, after all...?

He placed the mannequin back where he'd found it then continued along the passage to his bedroom.

Once inside, he went over to his bed, where he sat himself down on the mattress.

The sheets felt cold on his thighs.

Icy cold, as if they had not been slept in.

Had he really been gone that long?

At once he noticed his breath.

It was steaming in front of his face.

The air in the room was cold.

As cold as it had been in the Study.

The wind blew outside, and the curtains shook.

He got up from the bed and approached the window.

Parting the blinds, he saw that it was shaking on the latch.

It had recently been opened.

Mollat shook his head.

Was his mind playing more tricks on him?

He'd been standing there only minutes earlier.

The window had definitely been closed; he was certain of it.

A shiver ran up his spine.

There was someone else here...

A floorboard squeaked behind him but before he could turn to see who it was, he felt the bite of a rope against his windpipe.

The cord immediately tightened, and he felt the air being sucked from his lungs.

He reached up to grasp at the cord but couldn't work his fingertips beneath it.

He choked and gasped.

He felt the warm breath of his attacker on his neck.

"Don't struggle," a woman's voice said. "It'll only hurt more."

He struggled to free himself, but the more he moved, the tighter the noose became.

She raised her leg and planted her knee against his spine.

The cord suddenly drew tighter.

He couldn't breathe.

He needed to do something, otherwise he would be choked to death.

Suddenly, somewhere in the back of his mind a long-forgotten memory returned to the fore.

It was from his time in the military; a lesson he'd learned in basic training: what to do if you were attacked from behind.

At once he knew what to do.

He arched his back and took a pace backwards.

The movement caught his attacker off guard, and with her one leg raised, she fell backwards, crashing into the stanchion of his four-post bed.

Wood splintered and they fell down together on the floor.

As they dropped down, he twisted his body and bent his arm, driving his elbow into her ribs.

She squealed and let go of the rope.

Mollat quickly picked himself up and staggered toward the door, clawing at his neck to remove the noose.

He rushed out of the room and quickly made his way along the landing.

As he approached the stairwell, he managed to work his index finger beneath the cord. The rope slackened and he finally took a breath.

He looked over his shoulder towards the bedroom.

The woman was on her feet, standing at the doorway, her face and features shrouded in a dark cloak that covered her from head-to-foot.

To his surprise, she didn't chase after him.

Instead, she just stood there, watching him as he made his way down the stairs.

In the dimness of the moonlight, he saw the flash of a smile.

Wasting no time, he ran as fast as he could toward the door.

Just before his hand touched the handle, the rope around his neck tautened, and his legs were swept from under him.

He hit the floor hard, landing awkwardly on his shoulders.

He glanced up at the balustrade.

The woman was standing behind the rail, holding the trailing end of the rope in her hands. In a single swift movement, she threaded the line through the spindles of the bannister then pulled.

The pivot acted as a fulcrum, increasing her strength four-fold, and he was dragged backwards.

As he slid across the floor, he reached out for one of the boxes, thinking he could use it as a brace, but as his fingers touched it, the thing tipped over, and its contents spilled out over the floor.

In desperation, he grasped at the rope behind his head, but as soon as he took the line, it struck the panels of the wall beneath the balcony.

He heard a crack.

It was his fingers breaking.

His hand went numb with pain, but it was nothing compared to the sting of the cord that was biting deeper into his neck.

He turned his eyes upwards and saw the woman looking down at him.

"I told you not to fight," she rasped.

She planted the sole of her boot against the rail and hauled upon the line.

Mollat shrieked as he was hoisted up; first to feet, then up and off the floor.

The air was instantly sucked from his lungs.

He tried to breathe in but couldn't.

He panicked and struggled, scratching at the noose with both of his hands.

But it only made things worse.

The more he struggled, the tighter it became.

His heels kicked out beneath him, dancing the Hangman's jig.

He felt the blood pooling inside his head, starting at the back of his skull, then working forward through his temples, cheeks and around his eyes.

His vision blurred.

He eyes felt hot inside their sockets.

Everything was tinged with red.

He began to feel woozy, as if he was falling asleep.

Don't close your eyes, a voice inside his head rasped. *If you do, you'll die.*

But then a stronger voice called out to him.

A voice that told him everything was going to be ok and that all he needed to do was close his eyes...

Was it V'Loire?

For a moment, he was imbued with a sense of calm, a strange light-headed feeling; the kind he'd felt as a boy after drinking too much wine.

It was a warm feeling, a peaceful feeling...

A feeling of... *nothing at all.*

He suddenly forgot who he was.

The name he'd been given as a child vanished from his mind.

He realised that the life he so desperately clinging onto wasn't real.

Nor were his hopes, dreams, and anxieties.

His cares slipped away as he gave into the will of the soothing voice and closed his eyes....

CHAPTER 1

Dirk sat up in bed and wiped the trails of salt from his eyes.

The sun was rising outside, and its light was gently seeping through the slats of the blinds that covered his window.

There was a chill in the air, more reminiscent of winter than early autumn.

He pulled back the sheets and swung his legs over the side of the bed, then winced as he set them down on the cold stone floor.

He stood up and made his way over to the washbasin.

The water inside was murky and smelled of grime and soap.

It hadn't been changed in days.

It was his fault.

If he hadn't been so sniffy with Lottie, the housemaid, she wouldn't have refused to clean his room.

He'd have to bite his lip and apologise next

time he saw her.

He couldn't wash himself with dirty water forever.

Cupping his hands, he placed them inside the bowl and then quickly spooned the water over his face, head, and shoulders.

It was icy cold, and he shivered as he took his towel from the hook. After drying himself off, he soaped up his chin and began shaving his face. Once he's made himself look presentable, he tied back his hair and approached the small dresser that sat in the corner of his room. Other than his bed, it was the only furniture there.

It wasn't something he complained about.

At least he had his own room.

Compared to the shared dormitories of the Guildschool and the Ghisian Guildhouse, it was luxury living.

It didn't matter if it was small, cramped and unfurnished.

It was nice to have his own space.

After putting on his uniform, he left his quarters and went downstairs to the mess hall, where he joined Ing in the food line.

"What's being served today?" he asked.

The Rhunligger grinned.

"Sausages," he replied.

"Really?" Dirk echoed. "Who'd have thought..."

Ing laughed.

The Chief Cook at the Durnborg Guild was an

ex-serviceman named Heinrich. When it came to food, he had a limited repertoire. He could cook almost anything... as long as it came from a pig and was wrapped in an intestine. Under his supervision, the kitchen served sausages - and only sausages - morning, noon and night.

Not that anyone ever complained...

For Heinrich was known for his temper, and it was often shown if anyone criticised his cooking.

"Have you seen today's *Job Sheet*?" Dirk asked, as the line slowly shuffled forward.

The *Job Sheet* was a document produced each night by the Guildsergeant, Vargas, and contained a list of the day's assignments. Every morning, it was hung on a noticeboard outside the Mess Hall.

Ing nodded.

"We're on *pudding* this morning," he replied.

'Pudding' was Guildsman-slang for 'Picking Up Duty'. It involved bringing in criminals who'd abstained from their appearances in Court.

"How many perps?" Dirk asked.

"Just the one," Ing said, with a smile.

"Where does he live?"

"Krontsen House," Ing groaned. "But, on the bright side, at least it means we'll be back in time for lunch..."

* * *

After eating breakfast, Dirk and Ing left the

Guildhouse and made their way across town to the poor quarter, known colloquially as *'The Wash'*. The district was infamous for its ugly tenement buildings and the proliferation of ne'er-do-wells and petty thieves, who inhabited them.

Krontsen House was among them: a towering monstrosity of daub and timber, with rotting joists that separated each floor.

"Which flat is it?" Dirk asked, as they climbed the steps to the door, which hung broken on its hinges.

"Number eighteen," Ing replied, checking the warrant scroll. "It's on the top floor."

Dirk craned his neck upwards.

The tenement was seven storeys high.

"V'Loire..." Ing groaned. "So much for being back before lunch..."

They pushed open the door and made their way inside.

The lobby was dark and cluttered with rubbish. Though there was a large dumpster sitting outside, it seemed the residents seldom used it.

The air smelled of sewerage.

"Nice place," Ing noted. "...If you're a rat."

As they made their way over to the stairwell, Dirk wondered what it would be like to live here.

The conditions seemed awful; sanitation was non-existent.

It was a grim, depressing place.

It was hardly surprising that many of the residents turned to crime.

They turned up the stairs and began their long walk to the top floor. As they passed between each level, Dirk noticed people standing in the corridors. As soon as they noticed their Iron Seals, they rushed inside their apartments and locked their doors.

When Dirk and Ing reached the top floor, the Rhunligger stopped and puffed out his cheeks.

He was exhausted and needed a second to catch his breath.

He'd grown fat since *Passing Out* day, and his tunic hugged the bulge of his waistline.

"Wait a second," he said, panting. "I'm not used to this..."

"It's all the sausages and ale," Dirk mocked. "Maybe you should join me on my nightly run?"

Ing held up his hand.

"And miss out on precious drinking time?" he scoffed. "You do realise I chose this place for the nightlife..."

Dirk smiled.

Ing had never wanted a career in the Guild.

It had been forced upon him, as penance for his father's treason, and he spent most of his days dreaming of retiring to the country, where he would whittle away his pension on a steady diet of women and booze.

Ing wiped the sweat from his brow.

"Ok," he said. "I'm ready."

They made their way down the corridor and found the Perp's flat at the far end.

Dirk knocked on the door.

Inside, they heard a groan then footsteps approaching.

The handle turned and the door opened.

Standing before them was a man in his early thirties.

He had scruffy brown hair, which fell awkwardly over his ears. The skin of his cheeks and neck were unshaved. A ragged sheet was drawn across his shoulders. It was the only thing covering his modesty.

"Nye Yossell?" Dirk asked.

"Who's asking?" the man replied, belligerently.

Ing gave him a glance.

The man was trying to be funny.

"We're Guildsmen," Dirk said, formally. "We're here to escort you to the courthouse."

"For what?" the man spat.

"Unpaid taxes," Ing replied.

The man sniffed.

"There's no tax I've wanted to pay that I haven't," the man said, somewhat cryptically.

Dirk unfurled the scroll.

"It says here you missed the last three payments of the Citizen Standard."

The Citizen Standard was a poll tax that had been introduced the previous year. It was an unpopular levy, and opposition to it was rife.

"The Citizen Standard discriminates against the poor," the man replied. "How is it fair that a man who lives in a mansion should pay the same as someone who lives in a hovel?"

"We're not here to discuss politics," Dirk said. "Get your things. You're coming with us."

The man gestured to his attire.

"I can't go like this," he remarked. "What would the Magistrate say?"

Dirk looked him up and down.

It was true.

If he turned up to the court, looking the way he did, he'd probably face an additional charge of contempt.

"Fine," Dirk said. "But we're waiting inside."

"Suit yourself," the man sniffed.

He led them down a short hallway to a modest living area, which was only slightly bigger than Dirk's room at the Guild.

"Stay here while I put on my slacks," the man said, as he headed for the door which led to the bedroom.

"Be quick," Dirk warned. "...And no funny business."

The man groaned then disappeared through the door.

Dirk glanced at Ing, who was looking around the room.

"This place is disgusting," he remarked.

It was true.

The flat resembled a hovel.

It reminded him of the Shanty outside Ghis.

The floor was covered in junk and cuttings of

old carpet, the furniture was old and chipped, the walls were flaking and unpainted and there were ugly patches of mould growing around the window.

The only thing missing was a hole in the roof.

"I can't believe anyone would choose to live like this," Ing snorted. "Look at it. The whole place is filthy. He should hire himself a cleaner..."

"Maybe he can't afford it," Dirk replied.

"It costs nothing to keep things tidy," Ing remarked.

"True," Dirk replied, "But sometimes it's a case of finding the will to do it."

Having lived through poverty himself, he knew how easy it was to fall into bad habits. When money wasn't coming in, it caused worry, and worry led to hopelessness and malaise.

"It sounds like you feel sorry for him," Ing snorted.

"Maybe I do," Dirk replied.

"For his laziness?"

Ing sniffed.

He lacked Dirk's empathy, but then again, he'd never known what it was like to be poor. Ing had been raised on a large estate near Rhunlig, and his upbringing had been one of wealth and privilege. The biggest irony was he'd probably never cleaned a room in his life, yet here he was, criticising Yossell for not cleaning his.

"Anyway," Dirk said, "It doesn't matter what I think. He broke the Law. It's our duty to take him in."

Ing sulked.

"Shame," he said. "For a moment there I thought you were going to suggest we leave."

Dirk gave him a cursory look.

"Don't you want to bring him in?" he asked.

"The man's probably got lice," Ing replied. "I'd rather not catch them."

Dirk shook his head.

"What were you saying just now about laziness...?"

Ing grunted, his hypocrisy exposed.

Just then, they heard a scraping sound in the bedroom.

"What was that?" Ing asked.

Dirk approached the door.

"Yossell?" he said. "What are you doing in there?"

"Nothing," the man replied.

It sounded like a lie.

"Come out now," Dirk said.

Yossell didn't answer.

Dirk pushed against the door.

It was locked from the inside.

"Open up," he said. "We're coming in."

There was no response.

Dirk stepped back then struck the door with his heel.

The latch shattered and it swung open.

Dirk and Ing stormed in.

Yossell was nowhere to be seen.

Against the far wall was a sliding window.

The pane had been pushed open.

Ing smirked.

"Well, there's an overreaction if ever I saw one..." he remarked, hinted that the man had jumped to his death. "He was only looking at six months..."

Dirk rushed over to the window.

He stuck his head out and looked down onto the street below.

There was no sign of a body.

Just them, to his left, he heard the clanging of boots on metal. He turned his head towards the sound and saw Yossell two storeys below him, climbing down a ladder that had been fixed to the wall.

"He's using the fire escape," Dirk yelled. "Go downstairs and head for the alley. We'll cut him off."

Ing nodded then rushed towards the door.

Dirk lifted his leg onto the windowsill and stepped out onto the ledge.

"Stop where you are," he shouted down.

Yossell looked up at him and responded with a toothy grin.

Dirk was incensed.

He edged his way along the ledge, keeping his back firmly pressed against the wall.

The ladder was fixed to the wall beyond. It ran from the rooftop down the side of the building, where it ended abruptly ten feet above the ground.

He glanced down at the runner.

He'd nearly reached the bottom.

Dirk grunted with frustration then extended his left arm and took hold the hold of the ladder's side.

Gripping it tightly, he swung his right leg over the gap and planted it firmly upon the ladder's rung. Taking the other side with his right hand, he shifted his left leg across.

He looked down and saw Yossell dropping onto the street below.

Dirk needed to get down there, fast.

But he knew that if he climbed down rung-by-rung, the man he was chasing would be long gone.

He suddenly had an idea.

He lifted his right leg off the rung and pushed his instep into the ladder's side, then did the same with his left.

He took a breath then weakened his grip on the ladder's sides.

At once, he began sliding down.

Within seconds, he neared the bottom.

Just before the ladder's end, he pressed his palms firmly into the rails. It slowed his descent, and when he felt his legs slip off the rungs, he tightened his grip to stop himself.

He glanced down the alley and saw Yossell turning the corner.

He let go of the bars and dropped down onto the street below.

He landed snugly on the balls of his feet, then used the natural spring of his instep to push himself off into a sprint.

He rounded the corner in pursuit of his quarry and caught sight of him turning left, past the tenement's frontage.

Dirk smiled.

If Ing had managed to get down the stairs in time, he'd be waiting for him by the front door.

As Dirk turned the corner, he saw a flustered-looking Ing emerging from the front door, drenched in sweat.

He came down the steps and spread his arms wide to bar Yossell's escape.

The Perp dipped his head and charged into him with his shoulder.

The impact knocked Ing off his feet, and he landed flat on his back.

The man continued running, in the direction of the market.

Dirk glanced down at his fallen comrade.

"I'm fine," Ing yelled. "Get him!"

* * *

The marketplace was busy.

It was a week away from the *Erntfest*, the Festival of Harvest, and the plaza was packed with farmers, grocers and townsfolk.

Dirk dodged through the crowd in pursuit of Yossell, who was surprisingly nimble on his feet.

He darted left and right through the throng, skilfully avoiding the people who were milling around the stalls.

Dirk was less agile, and within seconds he'd clattered into an old lady who had been too slow in heeding his warning to move. He crashed into her shoulder, spinning her round on her heels, and the bag she was holding dropped to the floor and exploded.

Tomatoes, carrots and potatoes spilled out onto the street.

"My vegetables!" the woman screamed, aiming a slap at Dirk's face.

Under normal circumstances, he would have stopped, apologised, and helped her.

But he didn't have time.

Yossell was getting away.

He nudged her aside and carried on running, yelling at everyone to get out his way.

In response, the crowd parted, giving him a free run on the escapee, who had nearly reached the edge of the plaza.

The man glanced over his shoulder and cursed.

Then he veered to his right, towards a trailer containing a cartload of apples. Without so much as breaking his stride, he reached out a hand and flipped the latch that locked the tail board. Under the weight of its cargo, the panel sprung open, and the apples inside poured out onto the cobblestones.

They fell at Dirk's feet.

He trod on one and it squelched under his heel.

He lost his footing and his face crashed down into the fruit.

He picked himself up and wiped the pulp from his cheeks.

He looked up at the fleeing man, who had now cleared the market and was heading for the bridge. It marked the edge of the county. If he managed to get to the other side, Dirk would have no power to arrest him.

He grunted with frustration and punched the floor, striking one of the apples, which disintegrated with a loud squelch.

A crowd of people gathered around him.

Most appeared concerned for his wellbeing, but some appeared angry, including the owner of the cart, whose wares had been completely.

"Who's going to pay for this?" the man retorted. "That was my biggest crop of the summer!"

Dirk got to his feet, and the man bunted him in the chest.

He took the man's wrist and twisted it round.

The farmer yelped and the horse that was attached to his cart whinnied.

He suddenly had an idea.

"Write to the Guild," he said, as he dashed over to the front of the trailer and unhooked the horse from its harness. "They'll compensate you for any damages to your stock..."

He climbed up onto its back.

"...Or your horse."

He dug his heels into the stallion's sides. It thundered forwards, its hooves drumming loudly upon the cobbles.

Dirk guided it out of the square, down the avenue that led to the bridge.

Up ahead, he saw Yossell turning onto the crossing.

The man clearly thought he was no longer being followed, as he'd slowed down to a jog.

It was careless move, and Dirk would make him pay for it.

He yelled at his steed to go faster.

Yossell turned his head.

For a second, he appeared confused, but when he looked up at the rider and saw Dirk's face, he turned on his heels and began running across the bridge as fast as he could.

But by now Dirk's steed was in full gallop, and he'd closed the gap.

Leaning down over the saddle, Dirk extended his hand and swiped at the man's collar as his horse thundered past. The blow sent Yossell tumbling to the ground, where he rolled several times before coming to a stop.

Dirk slowed his steed then brought it to a stop.

Then he wheeled his horse around and glanced at the man lying on the floor.

"Are you hurt?" he asked.

Yossell groaned and clutched the back of his head.

"I'll live?" he snarled. "No thanks to you..."

Dirk swung his leg over the horse's back and dropped to the floor.

"I gave you a chance to come quietly," he replied. "But you chose to do things the hard way."

The man sneered.

Dirk reached down and picked him up off the floor.

"Nye Yossell," he said formally. "You're under arrest."

CHAPTER 2

The Durnborg County Courthouse lay in the provincial district and was only a short walk from the Guild. It was an old stone building, designed in the classic civic style, with a brace of cylindrical pillars that stood either side of its iron framed door.

They were met by two guards at the entrance who waved them inside.

"We've come to collect on a warrant," Ing said to the clerk, who peercd at them over the counter.

"Name?" the man said sharply.

"Nyc Yossell," Dirk replied, shunting the prisoner forward. "He's wanted for tax evasion."

He handed the warrant scroll to the Clerk, who unfurled the document in his hands.

After studying the words on the page, he folded up the scroll then opened a large black book that was sitting on his desk. He riffled through the pages before opening it up on a page that was headed with the letter 'Y'.

"Ahh, yes," he said to himself. "*Nye Yossell...*"

He picked up a quill that was sitting on his desk then slowly dipped the nib into an inkwell.

After tapping off the excess, he began scribing the date on the page.

When done, he produced a book of receipts from beneath the counter and opened it up on the desk.

Once more, he dipped his quill into the ink and repeated the process of logging the date.

Dirk noticed Ing tapping his heel on the floor.

He was getting impatient.

It was midday.

Dinnertime.

"How long's this going to take?" the Rhunligger asked.

The Clerk put down his pen and glared at him.

"As long as it takes," he replied sternly. "When you're spending the Emperor's coin every Dram must be logged. It's a precise and meticulous process."

"I understand that," Ing replied, "But can't you speed things up a little?"

The Clerk lifted his hand and scratched the wispy white whiskers that covered his chin.

"No," he replied, without looking. "It can't be rushed. If you're too impatient to wait, may I suggest a different career."

Ing's faced flushed red with fury.

He was about to say something to the man,

but Dirk jumped in.

"It's fine," he said. "Take as long as you need."

Ing baulked, dismayed by his response.

Dirk ignored him.

After his experience in Ghis, he was thankful that the Law was being properly observed, however inexpediently.

When the Clerk finally finished his paperwork, he put down his quill and rang a bell at his desk. Moments later, the doors leading to the Gaol opened, and out stepped two guards, who shackled Yossell's wrists.

"Take him to cell five," the Clerk said.

"When do I see my Lawyer?" Yossell replied, as the gaolers took him by the arms.

"Later this afternoon," the Clerk said, without looking up. "He'll be sent down to you when he arrives."

"When exactly?" Yossell asked.

"When he arrives," the Clerk repeated.

He gestured to the guards to take him away and they shunted Yossell through the doors which led to the cells.

"Well, that's the end of that," Ing snorted. "Can we get paid now?"

The Clerk sniffed, then pushed the receipt book across the desk.

"I'll need both of your signatures here," he said, pointing to a box next to Yossell's name.

He handed Dirk the quill, and he scribed his name on the page. He then passed it to Ing, who did the same.

After checking their scrawls, the Clerk nodded, then told them to wait while he collected their bounty from the safe.

He slowly got to his feet and made his way through a door, which lay behind the counter

"Bloody hell," Ing said. "These rules and regulations are ridiculous! No wonder taxes are so high when there's this much bureaucracy!"

Dirk smiled.

"Would you rather there were no rules at all?" he asked.

"I'd rather there were a lot less of them," Ing huffed. "Then we wouldn't have to wait around so long..."

The Clerk returned from the room with a sack of coin, which was emblazoned with the Emperor's seal.

"Here," he said, handing it to Dirk. "Seventy-Five Drams and fifteen Schillings exactly."

Dirk took the pouch and secured it to his belt.

"Thank you," he said.

The Clerk nodded then returned to his paperwork.

"Finally," Ing said. "Let's eat."

* * *

They made their way outside and began walking up the street to the Guild House.

The incident with the Clerk had left Ing in a

foul mood.

"Well, that was a waste of a morning," he groaned.

"What do you mean?" Dirk asked. "We caught our man and brought him to justice. It was a success."

Ing shook his head.

"How, exactly?"

Dirk gave him a cursory look.

"We both get paid ten Drams an hour," Ing continued. "The job this morning took us four hours. That means the Guild shelled out Eighty Drams to catch this idiot, but his bounty only brought in seventy-five."

"So, what's your point?" Dirk asked.

"We're five Drams down," Ing answered. "If every job we had was like this, the Guild would be out of business."

Dirk shook his head.

"We'd have been done a lot sooner if he'd have come quietly," he said.

"True," Ing replied. "But he didn't, and we made the mistake of chasing him."

"What are you trying to say?" Dirk said. "That we should let our warrants run?"

"If they're not worth our time or effort..." Ing replied.

Dirk laughed.

"We can't pick and choose our jobs," he said.

"Why not?" Ing said. "Tradesmen do. They wouldn't take on a job that left them out of pocket... And neither should we."

Dirk laughed.

"So, according to you, we're nothing but tradesmen?"

Ing nodded.

"We deliver a service," he said.

Yes," Dirk replied. "But the Guild is not a business..."

"How so?" Ing responded. "We bring in warrants for coin. That coin pays our wages."

There was a curious logic to what he was saying.

But it didn't make sense.

"If we were to pick and choose the warrants we took on," Dirk suggested, "the criminals would get wise to it and the crime rate would explode."

"Yes," Ing replied. "And then they'd have to pay us more to bring it down..."

"The Emperor would refuse," Dirk replied.

"How could he?" Ing countered. "When we're the only game in town?"

"He'd sooner go back to the old ways," Dirk laughed.

He was referring to the time before the *Finder's Covenant*, when Manhunters did the work of the Guild.

"What's wrong with that?" Ing said. "There's nothing bad about having a little competition?"

Dirk shook his head.

"And risk another *Purge*?" he replied.

Ing fell silent.

They'd both learned about the *Hunter's Purge* during their time in Guildschool. It was an event that took place half a century ago, following the kidnapping of the La Broqian Prince, Alfons. His father, King Albert had been so enraged by what had happened that he placed a bounty of a million Drams on the kidnapper's heads.

The huge sum piqued the interest of nearly every Manhunter in Ethren, and they swarmed upon Pendforte to compete for the prize.

The scramble led to carnage.

Not only were innocent people wrongly arrested, interrogated, and tortured, but the Manhunters themselves turned upon each other, in an effort to eliminate the competition. By the time Prince Alfons' kidnappers were caught and tried, only half their number had survived.

The aftermath left the Kingdoms painfully short of men to enforce the Law.

The rate of crime increased, and towns and even whole cities were plunged into chaos. Everyday governance switched from the Burgomeisters to the leaders of organised gangs, who grew so rich and powerful that not even the bravest Manhunters were willing to pursue them.

As the months progressed, the gangs grew bolder, and when King Osreich I was assassinated on the streets of Wernerliecht by a group known as the *Blue Swallows*, the Empire of Gerwald and the five Kingdoms of Westren were forced to put aside their differences to come up with a solution.

It came in the form of the *Finder's Covenant*, an agreement made with The Guild, which granted it exclusive rights to all new warrants, in return for an affordable, dependable, and well-manned, service.

The contract changed the profession of Man-hunting overnight; bounties were standardised and fixed to tariffs, Guildsman were professionally trained, and a code of conduct was introduced to boost integrity.

The results were swift.

Within six months, order had been restored in the Kingdoms, and the rulers of Ethren breathed a collective sigh of relief.

"Ok, maybe not," Ing replied, finally. "But it would be nice to be paid a little more."

Dirk laughed.

"Why," he mocked. "Do you think you're worth it?"

"Shut up," Ing replied, with a smile.

* * *

At the end of the street, they came to the Guildhouse, which stood on the corner of *Flescher's Lane*. It was a modest two-storey building, that more resembled a Tavern than a Barracks.

It didn't need to be anything more.

After all, Durnborg was a small town, and crime was seldom.

As they entered the Guildhouse, Ing's face

dropped.

"What's wrong?" Dirk asked.

"Do you smell that?" his friend replied.

Dirk sniffed the air.

"No," he said. "What is it?"

"Nothing," Ing said.

Dirk gave him a cursory look.

The other Guildsman sighed.

"It means we've missed lunch..."

They made their way upstairs to the office, where Dirk handed their bounty to Errol, the Guild Clerk, who placed it inside the safe.

"Where is everyone?" Ing asked, as Dirk signed the receipt.

It was an astute observation.

Other than Errol, the building appeared empty.

"They've all gone to the Mollat Estate," the ageing Clerk replied. "A body's been found."

"A body?" Ing exclaimed.

"Aye," Erroll said. "Mollat himself, from what I hear..."

"How did he die?" Dirk asked.

The Clerk shrugged his shoulders.

"Dunno..." he admitted. "But it can't have been natural if they've called in the Guild."

Dirk glanced at Ing, who rolled his eyes.

"You've got to be kidding," he said. "It's the other side of town. I'm not going all the way over there on an empty stomach."

"When did everyone leave?" Dirk asked Errol.

"They set out with the Burgomeister just after mid-morning," he replied.

"The Burgomeister?" Dirk sniffed. "What's it got to do with him?"

Akin to the role of Mayor, the Burgomeister's role was to govern the town and its surrounding boroughs. The incumbent was responsible for the budgeting of the city funds, civic expenditure, and local taxation.

The current Burgomeister was a man named Kohn Klept.

He'd won the last election on the back of a spirited campaign led by *The Imperial Post*, the Empire's state-sponsored newspaper. Dirk knew little of him, save for the fact he was a cunning linguist, whose rhetorical style often managed to convince people he was telling them something they didn't already know.

"No idea..." Errol responded. "Then again, I never thought to ask. I've enough problems of my own here..."

He gestured to the shelves behind him.

The files upon them were cluttered and disorganised.

In the grand scheme of things, it appeared a trivial matter, but the grim look on the Clerk's face suggested that, for him at least, it was akin to a matter of life and death.

"It probably has something to do with the *Erntfest*..." Ing suggested, dourly. "The event is held on Mollat's estate."

"We should head over there," Dirk said. "See if we can lend a hand?"

"I don't know..." Ing replied. "Would it be better if we stayed here?"

His tummy rumbled.

"After all, someone has to hold the fort..."

Errol beamed.

"Yes," he said. "You can stay and help me sort out these files..."

Ing glanced at the records behind him then groaned.

"Ok, I'll go," he said to Dirk, resignedly. "...But you're buying me lunch on the way back!"

CHAPTER 3

Mollat's Manor was sited to the south of Durnborg, and was fronted by a huge flat field, covering several acres. It was bordered to the West by the River Wynt, a tributary of the Rhund.

The late afternoon sun lingered in the sky as Dirk and Ing made their way through the meadow to the house, a huge mansion that had been built in the style of a La Broqian Chateaux.

"This Mollat fellow owns a lot of land," Dirk remarked, as he cast his eyes over the vast estate.

"He's one of the richest men in Gerwald," Ing replied.

"How did he make his fortune?" Dirk asked.

"Through his holdings. He owns half the leaseholds in the northern counties."

"That's a lot of rent," Dirk cooed. "How come I've never heard of him before?"

"Because he's a hermit," Ing replied. "They say he's not left his house in years... That he spends all of his days inside, doing nothing but counting his money..."

"He never married?"

"Not that I know of," Ing answered.

It was strange to think that such a man had not taken a wife. With wealth as vast as his, he would surely have had a plethora of admirers.

It seemed odd that he'd chosen to live alone.

But without knowing the man personally, it was hard to fathom why.

"What a life..." Dirk mocked.

As they neared the house, he noticed its unkempt state. Tiles were missing from the roof, the brickwork was pocked and broken, and the wall surrounding its courtyard was overgrown with vines.

"Maybe Mollat should have used some of his money sprucing up the place?" he remarked.

"He'd have never done that..." Ing chuckled. "The man was known as a churl and pinchfist. If you owed him money, he'd chase you for every Dram."

There was a bitterness to his tone.

It sounded personal.

"How do you know so much about him?" Dirk asked.

"My father had dealings with him before he died," Ing snorted. "But I'd rather not talk about it."

Beyond the wall was a small courtyard. A small path in the centre led up to the house. It was lined with bushes on either side.

They were overgrown and unpruned, deformed by time and neglect, and resembled nothing more than shapeless green blobs.

The whole place felt unowned and unloved.

It was as if it had been discarded and was in the process of being reclaimed by the plants.

They ascended the steps to the veranda, then pushed open the twin chestnut doors that graced the manor's facade. A large lobby lay within, cluttered with boxes, stacked one on top of the other. To the right of the hall, a grand staircase rose up to the first-floor landing, which was trimmed with an elegant balcony, crafted from oak.

Hanging from the balustrade was a cord of rope.

Dangling beneath it was the body of an old man.

A number of Guildsmen were examining the scene with the Coroner. Guildcaptain Hamm was observing in the corner. His nose was buried in a handkerchief to block out the smell. Dirk knew him as a passive and agreeable man, close to retirement age, and who was keen to serve out his last remaining months with as little incident as possible

Standing beside him was Burgomeister.

He was of a similar age, but his build was slimmer, his hair was darker, and he had a sloping forehead that was crested in a widow's peak.

The two men were talking.

"You needn't worry, Sire," Hamm said. "I can

assure you this matter will be resolved by day's end."

"I knew I could count on you Guildcaptain," the Burgomeister replied. "...And I'll be sure to pass on my compliments to the Guildmaster in Kronnig."

Klept smiled warmly, then bowed to the Guildcaptain before making his way to the door.

"You two," Hamm called, when he noticed them standing at the door. "Where have you been?"

They approached the Guildcaptain.

"Sorry we're late, Sir," Dirk said.

"We were delayed at the Courthouse," Ing added.

"Well, I'm afraid all the hard work's already been done," the Guildcaptain said. "As you can see, there's not much here to investigate."

He gestured to the body hanging from the noose.

"Oh well," Ing shrugged. "Back to the Guildhouse..."

"Actually, Sir," Dirk said. "Would you mind if we stayed a while?"

Hamm laughed.

"Be my guest," he chuckled. "If you can stomach the smell..."

He coughed into his handkerchief, which had been soaked in lavender.

Dirk gave the captain a nod, then made his way to the body.

"What were you thinking?" Ing exclaimed.

"You just cost us a free afternoon..."

Dirk shook his head dismissively.

Ing's laziness knew no bounds...

"...And now we have to spend it with him!"

He gestured to the corpse.

Its skin had turned green and its limbs appeared contorted beneath the folds of the nightgown.

"Looks like this has been a wasted journey," Ing groaned. "It's clear what happened. The old man did himself in."

Dirk turned to the coroner, who was examining the corpse's toes.

"When did he die?" he asked.

"Judging by the level of rigor mortis..." he replied. "I'd say last night, between nine and ten."

Dirk looked up at the body and hummed.

"What are you thinking?" Ing asked.

"I'm not sure," Dirk replied, "But it's strange that a man who would do this to himself would go to the trouble of getting himself ready for bed...."

Ing fell silent.

"Maybe we should a stay a little while longer..." he said.

* * *

They made their way upstairs and leant over the rail to inspect the noose.

The knot was firm and secure.

"Have you ever tied one of these?" Ing asked.

"No," Dirk replied, "But I've been on the end of one..."

He shuddered at the memory.

Whilst working in Ghis he'd been set upon by a mob in the *Weidenslosse.*

They'd lynched him from a tree, and he'd been lucky to escape with his life.

Dirk inspected the rope.

It had been wound around the rail and its tail stretched backwards across the landing into the bedroom, where it had been secured to the leg of a large four-poster bed.

Dirk's eyes drifted to the bedding above the mattress.

The sheets had been folded over.

It had been slept in.

As he walked around the bed, he noticed a large crack in the post nearest the window.

"What do you make of this?" he asked.

"It's broken," Ing remarked. "Like the rest of this house."

Dirk crouched down.

"There are chippings of wood on the floor," he said. "This happened recently."

"Maybe it happened when he threw himself over the rail?" Ing suggested.

"If that was the case, why would this side snap?" Dirk replied.

He leant against the post.

The bed was heavy and sturdy.

He glanced down at the floorboards.

There were no scratches in the wood next to the bed's feet.

"The bed hasn't moved," he said.

"So, what caused the damage? Ing asked.

Dirk inspected the splintered post.

The break in the wood was at chest height.

"It's been hit with something heavy," Dirk said.

"What, like a mace?" Ing chuckled.

"Maybe," Dirk said, touching the point of his shoulder against the split. "Or a body."

"What are you saying?" Ing said.

"There was a struggle," Dirk replied, "A fight."

He stepped back and surveyed the scene.

"Someone was pushed into the bedpost."

Ing stroked his chin.

"If that's the case, how did they get in?"

Dirk made his way over to the curtains and opened them.

Behind them was a large window.

Dirk inspected the glass.

He noticed that the latch had been twisted, and that part of the wood was missing from it frame.

"What do you think happened here?" Dirk asked.

"It looks like someone jimmied the lock."

Dirk nodded.

"And I'd wager it was the same person who fought with Mollat and strung him up."

Ing groaned.

"So, you're saying this wasn't suicide?"

Dirk shook his head.

"It was murder," he said. "We should tell Hamm."

* * *

Hamm shook his head dismissively.

"As far as I'm concerned this matter is closed," he huffed. "Mollat hanged himself, plain and simple."

"But what about the break-in?" Dirk replied.

"One broken window does not a burglary make..." Hamm declared. "Especially in a house that is falling apart."

"There was evidence of a struggle in the bedroom," Dirk countered.

"Burglars usually steal..." Hamm replied.

He gestured to the boxes stacked around the room. All of them were overflowing with trinkets and treasures.

"...But nothing here has been taken."

"Maybe it wasn't a burglary?" Dirk suggested.

"Then what was it?" Hamm replied. "A murder?"

Dirk gave him a knowing look.

The Guildcaptain responded with a roll of his eyes.

"A murder requires a motive," he said. "Do you have one?"

Dirk shrugged his shoulders.

"I'm working on it," he replied.

The Guildcaptain shook his head.

"Don't waste your time," he said. "It seems patently clear to me why this man died."

He glanced at Mollat's body, which was being placed onto a gurney by the Coroner.

"He was lonely," Hamm said. "But instead of waiting for death to take him, he met it square on."

"But that doesn't fit the facts," Dirk replied. "We need to make more inquiries. We need to find out what *really* happened..."

The Guildcaptain puffed out his cheeks.

"You'll do no such thing," he huffed. "You'll return to the Guildhouse right away and write all this up. I want a full report on my desk before supper."

* * *

"You need to choose your battles," Ing said, as they made their way back through the garden. "You nearly earned us an extension."

Once they'd taken their vows of service, Guildsmen were committed to twenty-five years of service, but days, weeks, or sometimes even months were added to this period, usually as punishments for minor discretions.

Dirk let out a frustrated sigh.

"He's a blind old fool," he rasped.

"He's set in his ways," Ing replied. "He's worked in Durnborg so long, he thinks murders can't happen here."

"How can we make him change his mind?" Dirk asked.

"It'll be hard," Ing replied. "We need more evidence. Everything we have right now is circumstantial... It doesn't prove anything."

Dirk hissed under his breath.

As hard as it was to admit, everything Ing said was true.

"You need a distraction," Ing suggested. "Something to take your mind off things..."

"Such as?" Dirk snorted.

"I don't know..." Ing began. "Maybe invite Lottie on a stroll around the park? I've been told she likes you."

"Lottie likes anything in a uniform," Dirk replied. "That's why she works at the Guild."

Ing guffawed.

"What difference does that make?"

Dirk shook his head.

"I've a feeling we're not on best terms at the moment..."

Ing smirked.

"Are you talking about what happened last week?"

Dirk nodded.

He'd been sharp with her when she'd brought him his linen.

His slacks hadn't been properly pressed, and he'd told her to take them back.

She'd refused, arguing they were fine, but he

wouldn't back down, and she'd started to cry.

He hadn't meant to hurt her feelings.

He'd been bored and had taken his frustrations out on her.

It had been a stupid thing to do and he'd immediately regretted his actions...

But up until now he'd been too embarrassed to apologise.

"Maybe I should tell her I'm sorry?" he said.

"I would," Ing said. "Otherwise, you'll be wearing creased slacks for the next twenty-four years...."

Dirk laughed.

He pushed open the gate.

A woman screamed on the other side.

Dirk and Ing stepped outside to find an elderly woman clutching her chest. The shock had sent her tumbling backwards into the post box, and it has sprung open, spewing a clutch of letters onto the floor.

"You boys!" she said, between breaths. "You gave me such a fright!"

"Sorry," Dirk said. "We didn't see you there."

"Too many vines..." Ing added.

The woman puffed out her cheeks and composed herself.

"I remember the days when gentlemen were gentlemen," she said, "...and announced themselves in a presence of a lady. It's rude to sneak up on people..."

Ing glanced at Dirk.

His lips weren't laughing.

But his eyes were...

"We didn't mean to startle you," he said. "We're Guildsmen."

"I can see that!" she hissed. "Those awful grey tunics are hard to miss... What I want to know is why you're here? Is Kurgen in some kind of trouble?"

Ing inhaled sharply.

Dirk had a feeling that two shocks in one morning would be a little too much for her.

"Let's start with you," he said.

"Me?" she replied. "But what have I done? I'm just his seamstress."

"We're not accusing you of anything," Dirk said. "We just want to know why you're here."

She reached into the bag that was slung over her shoulder and produced a cushion cover.

"It had a tear in it," she said. "He wanted it stitched."

Ing smirked.

"And he was willing to pay you?"

The woman looked insulted.

But Dirk understood the point he was making.

Mollat was known skinflint.

It seemed unlikely he'd part with his coin for something as trivial as a torn pillow.

"Did he not have his own needle and thread?" Ing pressed.

"He did," the woman answered. "But it's not

as if he could do it himself..."

"Why not?" Ing asked.

"Because of his apoplexy," she replied.

Dirk knew of the condition.

His mother had died from it.

Even as a young boy he'd realised how serious it was.

It had struck her on the night, suddenly and without warning. Her face had dropped on the one side and she couldn't lift her arm. Come morning she was not the woman he knew, and a week after that she'd died in his father's arms.

The physician who'd visited then had told them she'd been lucky, as he'd seen others who had not been spared the mercy of death, and had been left crippled for life, with limbs that hung dead by their sides.

"Could he not hold a needle?" Dirk asked.

The woman shook her head.

"With his left hand, he could" she said. "But it takes two hands to sew."

Or tie a noose, Dirk thought.

"Well?" the woman said. " I've answered all your questions... Will you *kindly* let me through?"

Dirk sighed.

"I'm afraid I've some bad news," he said. "Mollat's dead."

The old woman scrunched up her face.

"Well, you could have told me sooner!" she hissed.

"Are you not upset?" Dirk asked.

"Only about my wasted thread..." she spat, stuffing the cushion back inside her bag.

She huffed, turned on her heels, then started walking away.

Dirk looked at Ing.

"So, it was definitely murder..." he said.

"How do you figure that?" Ing replied.

"The noose," Dirk said. "There's no way he could have tied it with one hand."

"True," Ing admitted. "But we're still missing a suspect... "

Dirk suddenly noticed the tranche of letters at the foot of the post box.

"You'd think a man as despised as Mollat wouldn't get many letters..." he remarked.

"It's probably all hate mail..." Ing chuckled.

Dirk smiled.

"Then let's see who hates him..."

He crouched down and gathered up the envelopes, then handed half of the bundle to Ing.

"What are we looking for?" Ing asked, as he took out the first letter and began scanning the page.

"I'm not sure," Dirk replied.

He flicked through the correspondence in his hands.

Most of the letters related to Mollat's rented properties, receipts, promissory notes, and whatnot.

Nothing looked out of order.

It seemed like a wasted endeavour.

Until he suddenly came across a letter that had been sent from the Office of the Burgomeister.

He removed the letter from the sleeve and read the words on the page.

"Dear Mr Mollat," it began, *"Please extend me the courtesy of reconsidering my offer to defer payment on this year's field rental. The Erntfest is the biggest event in the Provincial Calendar, and it is important to the people of Durnborg. It would be a terrible tragedy to see it cancelled over the matter of ten thousand Drams."*

It was signed at the bottom, *"Yours truly, the Office of Kohn Klept, Honourable Burgomeister of Durnborg and Durnborgschaft County."*

Dirk smiled.

"What is it?" Ing said.

"I think we have our suspect," Dirk replied.

He handed the note to Ing.

"V'Loire," the Rhunligger gasped. "You really think the Burgomeister had something to do with this?"

"I'm not sure," Dirk replied, "But there's no doubt he gained from Mollat's death. Maybe should we pay him a visit?"

CHAPTER 4

The Town Hall stood at the edge of Durnborg's main square. It was an impressive three-storey building with a flat roof, whose frontage was lined with concrete pillars. A large garden had been built around its side and rear, which was surrounded by a brick wall, ten feet high.

With its stone-grey facade, it looked more like a fortress than a building made for the public, but there was a certain beauty in its design that lent it an aura of majesty amongst the daub-and timber structures that stood on either side.

"It used to be a theatre," Ing remarked, as they made their way toward its imposing twin doors. "...Back when Plays were a thing."

Dirk had been too young to remember Plays.

They'd been banned throughout the Empire at the turn of the century, following a particularly rampant outbreak of a disease known as *The Flaming Death*. The court physicians had advised the

Emperor to close down the theatres to stop the virus from spreading. He'd duly obliged, but after the epidemic had abated, the showhouses never reopened, and when the playwrights and actors complained to the Royal Court, their pleas fell on deaf ears.

Most of the theatres fell into disrepair or were bought and demolished to make way for houses and tenements, but some, like this one, were converted and reborn in a different guise.

They went inside and found the lobby crowded with people.

They were here for the *Schaftmoot*, a weekly address made by the Burgomeister to the Citizens of the County.

Dirk and Ing pushed their way through the throng to the auditorium, where they found Klept addressing the audience.

"What do we do?" Ing asked. "We can't drag him off the stage."

Dirk nodded in agreement.

"We'll have to wait until he's finished," he replied.

He glanced around the hall, looking for somewhere to sit.

All the seats had been taken.

"Come on," he said. "We'll find somewhere to stand at the back."

They made their way over to the apron and found an empty space near the aisle between two farmhands.

The men tipped their hats as they approached.

"Are you here to learn about the Erntfest?" one of them asked.

"Possibly," Dirk replied, somewhat cryptically.

He turned his head to the stage.

Klept was speaking to the crowd from behind a tall lectern, which was emblazoned with the Emperor's seal. He was wearing his dark green robes of office and looked to be in his element, jostling with the crowd like a troubadour.

"After the morning parade," he declared, "There'll be a market in the afternoon, followed by the traditional evening bonfire."

The audience responded by clapping excitedly.

"In accordance with tradition," he added, "may I ask that everyone who attends bring along a log for the pyre, so that the flames continue to burn throughout the night."

"What about drinks?" someone shouted.

"Ah," Klept said, tipping his head. "I'm glad you asked, for I've just received word that the Royal Brewery have donated ten kegs of Grott's Ale for the party."

The crowd cheered.

"...The *Durnborg Dodgers* will also be in attendance to help you drink it," he added. "After last week's defeat, they'll be more than happy to share their lament."

Several groans emanated from the crowd.

The *Durnborg Dodgers* were the town's *Kick Ball* Team. They'd recently made it to the final of the Emperor's Cup but had lost the match in extra time, thanks to a fluke drop-goal.

"Bloody Dodgers," Ing remarked. "They cost me thirty Drams!"

Like many other Durnborgers, he'd placed a bet on the Dodgers to win, but the bookies had been the only people cheering at the final whistle...

"You'll also be treated to an exhibition from the champion prize-fighter, Ralph Olberwalt," Klept continued. "I hear he's willing to take on all comers, so sign up... if you feel brave."

He then finished on a more sombre note.

An obituary.

"As most of you may already be aware," he began, "a dear friend of ours died last night. His name was Kurgen Mollat. Some of you may know him as a landlord, a leaseholder, or as a business partner, but to me and everyone else, he was the man that made the *Erntfest* possible and will continue to do so in years to come."

The hall fell into a revered silence.

"And so, with his passing," Klept continued, "I propose that from this year and every year forthwith, we rename the cake stall in his honour."

His suggestion was met with muted applause.

It was clear that Mollat was unpopular and his death didn't matter to them.

A VOW OF SUCCOUR

It saddened Dirk to think people could be like this.

Though no one really liked him, he was still one of them.

It reminded him of the attitude that had been taken by the authorities to his own father's death.

Like Mollat, Minas had been a nobody.

And like Mollat, his death didn't matter.

Dirk snorted angrily.

"Are you ok?" Ing asked.

"I'm fine," Dirk replied.

But inside, he was fuming.

When the crowd stopped clapping, the Burgomeister stepped away from the lectern and opened the floor to questions.

A female scribe, at the end of the row raised her hand.

She was wearing a blue tunic, which featured the emblem of the *Durnborg Standard,* the town's local rag.

Klept gestured for her to speak.

"Sire," she began, "Regarding the *Erntfest*... How can you assure us it will go ahead, given that the Guild are still investigating Mollat's death?"

The question sent ripples of consternation through the hall.

"As I alluded to earlier," the Burgomeister began, "His death is not being treated as suspicious. I've been given personal assurance by the Guildcaptain himself that his men will leave the site by the end of the day, therefore, I can assure you that the *Erntfest* will go ahead as planned."

"Is this like when you *assured* us, you'd scrap the Poll Tax?" someone shouted out.

Dirk looked toward the voice and saw a man standing in the far aisle.

He looked like he came from *The Wash*, as his clothes were ragged.

Upon his head was a blood-red chaperon.

It was the uniform of the *Scarlet Faction*, a group of political dissenters who were fielding a candidate against Klept in the forthcoming election.

Dirk knew little of them save for the fact that they were radicals, who wanted to replace the Monarchy with what they called a *'People's Council'*.

The state-owned *Imperial Post* had decried the organisation and its members as 'extremists' and 'loons', unworthy of serious consideration.

But despite this, the man's words seemed to be resonating with the audience, who were grumbling in agreement.

Dirk glanced at the Burgomeister, who looked nervous and uncomfortable.

"The promise I made in regard to the Citizen's Standard were true at the time I made them," he responded, somewhat cryptically. "But circumstances changed..."

"How?" the man in the red hat replied.

"There were additional costs," Klept replied. "Unforeseen expenses."

The man laughed out loud.

"What 'additional' costs?" he retorted. "No extra alms have given to the poor houses, you've frozen the pay of civil servants, and you've nothing to fix the sewers in the Eastern quarter..."

Dirk saw many people in the crowd nodding their heads.

"...So, tell us, *Burgomeister*," the man rasped indignantly, "What happened to all the money?"

The words clearly riled Klept, who glared at the man wickedly.

"What do you know of managing a County's budget?" he countered. "If it was up to you, you'd squander it all."

"We'd help the poor and downtrodden," the man replied. "Not ourselves."

His words were greeted with murmurs of agreement.

Dirk sensed that the hall was quickly turning against Klept.

The Burgomeister needed to win them over, fast.

But instead, he smiled nervously, then called an end to the meeting.

"No more questions," he declared. "This *Schaftmoot* is over."

He then stormed off stage to a series of boos from the audience.

The people in crowd seemed incensed.

Some of them stood up and urged him to come back.

Others tutted and shook their heads.

"There's your motive," Ing laughed. "If the Erntfest ends up being cancelled, not even the *Three-Armed Monster* could save him..."

He was referring to the Press, Church and Academies, who were backing Klept's re-election. Together they worked in harmony to preserve the status quo, acting as the voice, heart and mind of the Emperor.

It was said a candidate endorsed by the triumvirate was guaranteed success.

But after witnessing what had just happened, Dirk wasn't so sure.

"Do you think he'll be in the mood to talk after what just happened?" Ing asked with a grin, as the people in hall got up from their seats and started making their way out.

Dirk smiled wickedly.

"It's a shame he doesn't have a choice..."

* * *

Once the hall had cleared, Dirk and Ing made their way down to the apron, where they climbed the stairs up to the stage, and traced the Burgomeister's footsteps through a passage that lay beyond the left wing. Stepping through, they found themselves in a narrow run which led to a series of dressing rooms that lay behind the curtain.

"Where do you think he went?" Ing asked.

Dirk looked at the doors.

Each one had been labelled.

The one at the end read, 'Burgomeister'.

"There," Dirk said, pointing it out.

They walked toward it.

As they closer they heard talking inside.

One of the voices was definitely Klept. The other was deeper, and more heavily accented.

"He has company," Dirk noted. "They sound like they're arguing..."

"What's the betting they're his supporters?" Ing laughed.

Suddenly there was a loud crashing sound inside.

Dirk glanced at Ing, then pushed open the door.

They rushed in to find Klept being throttled by a huge Half-Ogre. The beast had pinned him against the wall. A Dwarf wearing a gold chaperon, stood behind them with his arms were crossed over his chest.

"Put him down," Dirk ordered, reaching for his sword.

The Ogre turned his head, then looked to the Dwarf for instruction.

The Halfling nodded and the brute released his grip.

The Burgomeister slid down the wall and dropped to his knees.

"What's going on here?" Ing barked.

"Nothing," the Dwarf replied. "We were just leaving."

"No, you're not," Dirk spat. "We're placing you

both under arrest."

"No, No.." the Burgomeister said, as he stood up and patted himself down. "...There's no need for that. These are friends of mine."

Ing laughed.

"They don't look like it," he remarked.

"Well, they are," Klept replied.

"Friends don't choke each other," Dirk said.

The Burgomeister forced a smile.

"Is that what it looked like?" he replied, his voice aghast. "He was merely helping me with my hood."

The Dwarf grinned, triumphantly.

"We'll be seeing you round, Koln," he rasped, then made his way to the door, with the Ogre following behind.

Dirk kept his eyes on them as they left.

When they had gone, he turned back to Klept, who had gotten to his feet and was adjusting his collar.

"Sorry about that," he said. "You meet all sorts of people working in politics..."

"The same can be said for working in the Guild," Dirk replied.

"Quite right," the man replied.

He sat himself down at his desk and began mopping the sweat from his forehead with his sleeve.

"So," he began, "I take it you're here to inform me of your progress?"

"Not quite," Dirk replied.

The man gave him a cursory look.

"But the investigation is complete, is it not? The Guildcaptain assured me that Mollat's death would be considered a suicide."

"It's not as simple as we first thought," Dirk replied. "there's evidence to suggest Mollat was murdered."

The Burgomeister's face turned white.

"Murdered?" he exclaimed. "But he hanged himself."

"Not necessarily," Dirk replied. "But it was made to look that way."

"Really?" Klept scoffed. "And what makes you say that?"

"A number of things," Dirk replied. "We found evidence of a break in upstairs, and we have a witness who claims Mollat couldn't have tied the noose."

The Burgomeister sniffed.

"What man can't tie a knot?" he huffed.

"A man who only had the use of one arm," Dirk replied.

He took a step forward.

"We also found some interesting letter in his post box," he added, looking into the Burgomeister's eyes. "Letters from your office... Begging letters, asking him to waive the fee for the rental of his field."

Klept held his gaze.

"So?" he replied. "It is not my civic duty to get the best deal for my citizens?"

"Where we you last night?" Dirk asked.

"I was at the Count's Reception," the man answered.

"What time did you get there?" Dirk pressed.

"Six," Klept replied.

"When did you leave?" Ing asked.

"After midnight," he replied.

"And were you there the whole time?"

"Yes."

"Do you have any witnesses to prove it?" Dirk asked.

"Many," the man replied.

"Give us some names."

The Burgomeister puffed out his cheeks.

"Am I being accused of something here?" he said.

"You tell me," Dirk replied.

"I'd rather not," Klept said. "You're the ones with the Iron Seals."

He looked them up and down.

"...Though it's plain to see you've not been wearing them long. Did Hamm send you?"

Ing gave Dirk a nervous glance.

Klept caught him looking.

"...Maybe I should speak with him about this? Cut out the middle...*boys*?"

"Maybe we should go?" Ing said to Dirk.

He looked uncomfortable, as if his tunic was tightening around his neck.

The Burgomeister smiled wickedly.

The boot was now on the other foot.

"Yes," he suggested. "Maybe you should."

Dirk looked at Ing.

His face was bright red.

"Perhaps I should take your names?" Klept said. "...So I can follow up this matter with your Guildsergeant?"

"No," Dirk replied. "It's fine. We're going."

Gritting his teeth, Dirk followed Ing to the door.

"Oh, and next time you come snooping around my offices," Klept sneered, "...make sure you have a warrant."

* * *

The hard rain falling did little to dampen Dirk's fury, as they crossed the town square.

He was angry that Klept had outsmarted them.

The man was a murderer.

He was sure of it.

But their interrogation of him had proven fruitless.

"Let's visit the Count," Dirk said. "Let's see if Klept's alibi holds up?"

"What about Hamm?" Ing replied. "We promised him the report by supper."

Dirk shook his head.

"It's not going to happen," he said. "The investigation isn't over."

"According to him, it is..." Ing replied.

Dirk puffed out his cheeks.

"If we write that report," he said. "It means letting Klept get away with murder..."

Ing shrugged.

"What else can we do...?"

CHAPTER 5

"You want what?" Hamm retorted, slamming his palm down on the desk.

"A warrant, Sir," Dirk replied. "To speak to Klept. He says he won't talk to us without one."

"And neither should he!" the Guildcaptain snorted.

He placed his hand in his pocket and took out a handkerchief, which he used to wipe the sweat from his moustache.

"I can't believe the two of you defied my orders," he snorted. "Did I not make myself perfectly clear at the manor? You were to return here immediately to write up the report."

"You did, Sir," Dirk admitted.

"Then why did you go to the town hall to harass the Burgomeister?"

"We're sorry, Sir," Ing replied. "We'll complete the report right away."

"Oh, I don't think so," Hamm declared. "I'm

taking both of you off the case. Moreover, for the next two weeks, you're confined to the Guild, where I'm placing you under Errol's charge in Records. You can help him sort out his files..."

"But Sir," Dirk implored. "We know Klept's guilty. Allow us to arrest him and we'll deliver a confession."

"Guilty of what?" the Guildcaptain asked.

"Mollat's murder," Dirk replied.

Hamm buried his face in his hands.

"There was no murder," he replied. "The old man killed himself, plain and simple."

"He couldn't have, Sir," Dirk replied. "There's no way he could have tied the noose."

Hamm snorted through his nose.

"Why?" he asked. "Did he have an aversion to knots?"

"He'd had a stroke, Sir," Dirk replied. "He only had the use of one arm."

The Guildcaptain huffed.

"Says who?" he replied. "Not Mollat, that's for sure. If I remember correctly, the last time I saw him, he was dead..."

"His seamstress told us, Sir," Dirk replied. "We questioned her outside."

He reached inside his tunic and produced the letter they had found in Mollat's post box.

"We also found this," he added.

He handed Hamm the note.

"...It suggests Mollat was in dispute with the council."

The Guildcaptain took the note and gave it a cursory look before dropping it onto the table.

"This proves nothing," he said.

"It proves motive, Sir," Dirk replied. "Klept needed that field. Without it the *Erntfest* would have been cancelled, and it would have left him at the mercy of the voters."

Hamm's face softened, and for a second it looked as if his mind had turned.

But then he grimaced and shook his head.

"No," he said dismissively. "I can't accept this. I've known Klept for fifteen years. He's a good man, a loyal man, a man who only wants the best for this nation. He wouldn't go around murdering people."

Dirk shook his head.

"You're mistaken," he replied.

Hamm stood up.

"No," he yelled. "You are!"

He began pacing around the room.

"I'm aware of what happened to you in Ghis," he said, pointing a finger at him, "but you need to understand that things are different here. This isn't some backwater cesspit, where corruption is rife and everything bad that happens is the result of some *heinous* intent..."

He went over to the window and looked out through the glass at the serene streetscape beyond.

"This is Durnborg," he opined. "A place where nothing happens..."

He turned his head and looked Dirk in the

eye.

"...And I refuse to believe things have changed overnight."

* * *

The records room was cluttered and untidy, with bundles of paperwork stacked up along the walls.

"Every document has to be filed according to its type and status," Errol had told them, before he'd left for supper. "Closed warrants go in the 'D' section, whilst Receipts are filed on the second shelf, under 'W', beneath the arrest lists, which are all marked with the letter 'R'."

"Wouldn't it make more sense to file arrests under 'A'?" Dirk suggested.

"'A' is already used to denote 'Absconders'," the Clerk had replied snootily.

"What about 'R'?" Ing had asked.

"'R' is a legacy issue, from the previous system. Although we still use the shelf for an overspill of warrants if 'D' fills up..."

The system seemed confusing and made little sense, but despite their protestations, Errol had assured them they would 'soon pick things up', and if they got stuck, to jot down any queries, which he would 'answer later'.

It was an hour after supper.

The Clerk had yet to return, and their list of queries was two pages long and growing by the minute.

"Where do you think he is?" Dirk asked.

"Probably at *The Glass* with everyone else..." Ing sighed.

The Glass was a tavern on *Tomas Lane*. It was where most Guildsmen went drinking after finishing their shift.

Ing loved the place as they served his favourite drink, a malty ale called, *Grersons*. It was brewed in his hometown of Rhunlig, and it reminded him of home.

"He'll be there all night," Dirk mused.

"While we're stuck here..." Ing replied.

He looked annoyed.

Dirk could tell he was still mad at him.

"I'm sorry for getting you into trouble," he said, as he picked up a stack of arrest lists and began sorting them by name.

"It's ok," Ing shrugged. "It could have been a lot worse."

It was true.

Defiance of orders was a technical breach of their vows.

The punishment for this could be harsh, as he'd learned to his cost in Einhof, but Hamm was known for his light touch.

In Dirk's ten months' service in Durnborg, the biggest sanction applied by Hamm had been a weeks' extension to Hogar's service, and that had been for stealing evidence that implicated his wife in the theft of an apple pie.

Hamm had blustered over it for days.

He'd called briefings about it, arranged for the men to attend mandatory lessons, and had brought each trooper into his office to stress the importance of maintaining their integrity.

But in the end, the consequences for Hogar had been piffling.

A mere seven days.

Hamm had proven himself to be all bark and no bite.

No wonder the men called him, 'toothless'...

"If he'd have found out we'd gone to the Count to check on his alibi," Ing continued, "we'd have got a lot longer than two weeks."

Dirk shrugged.

Maybe three, he thought.

"It would have been a wasted journey, anyway," Ing added.

"Why do you say that?" Dirk asked.

"Because no one would use a party as a false alibi," Ing replied. "There would have been too many witnesses."

"Are you saying Klept didn't do it?" Dirk asked.

Ing laughed.

"I think he's guilty as sin," he replied.

Dirk looked at him, confused.

"How?" he sniffed. "No man can be in two places at once."

"Who said he needed to be?" Ing replied.

Of course, Dirk thought.

It suddenly seemed obvious.

Klept hadn't done the dirty work himself... He'd hired someone else to do it for him.

"A contract killer," he said aloud.

"Yes," Ing confirmed. "But there's a problem with that theory."

"What?" Dirk asked.

"Klept couldn't afford it."

During his training, Dirk had learned about organised crime, and the typical costs the syndicates would charge for burglaries, thefts and assassinations. The standard price for a gangland execution was fifteen thousand Drams... Five thousand more than the cost of Mollat's field.

Dirk sighed.

"Looks like we've hit a brick wall..." he said.

Ing didn't reply.

Dirk glanced over at him.

The Rhunligger was reading one of the files.

"Maybe not," he said.

"What is it?' Dirk asked.

Ing removed the record from the folder and tossed it over.

Dirk caught it and held it up into the light.

It was a *Charge Sheet*, a document created by the Courts whenever someone had been arrested. Copies were shared with the Guild.

"Ertha Rouge?" he said, reading aloud the name that had been scribed at the top.

"A hired Killer," Ing replied. "She works for Ruul Zamar."

Ruul Zamar ran *The Night Owls*, the Empire's largest syndicate. They were based in the capital, Royal Kronnig, and were one of the few organisations to have eluded the Guild since the end of the *Hunter's Purge*.

"The Guard picked her up three nights ago, just outside Berghof," he answered.

"That's only a few miles north of here," Dirk noted. "Why was she arrested?"

"Breaking her parole," Ing replied. "She was subject to a travel bans, which prevented her from leaving the capital."

"So, what was she doing in Berghof?"

Ing gestured to the file.

"She claims she was attending her father's funeral."

Dirk smirked, then turned his eyes to the page.

"It says here she was released yesterday afternoon..." he said. "...that the charges were rescinded, and she was freed."

"Who signed the order?" Ing asked.

Dirk recognised the signature.

"Kohn Klept," he replied.

Ing's eyes widened.

"How did I know it was going to be him...?" he groaned.

Dirk glanced down the page.

"It says, here, that she had an outstanding warrant for the murder of a horse dealer from Bruun."

"How did they die?" Ing asked.

Dirk read the notes.

"Strangulation," he replied.

He turned over the file and handed it back to Ing.

The Rhunligger studied it with his eyes.

"She sure sounds like our girl," he said.

"Do you think Klept cut her a deal?" Dirk asked.

"I'd say so," Ing replied. "She was facing the death penalty."

"We need to bring her in," Dirk said. "Ask he what she knows."

Ing laughed.

"Mollat was killed last night," he said. "By now she's probably back in the capital, lauding it up in Ruul's palace."

"Then we'll go to Kronnig and get her," Dirk replied.

"And do what?" Ing replied. "Ask her nicely to come with us? You're forgetting our powers of arrest end at the county line."

Dirk sighed.

It was true.

The 'Boundaries of Jurisdiction' was a clause in the *Finders Covenant*, which prevented any Guild from operating outside its home county. It's inclusion in the agreement had been a controversial one, as it allowed people to escape justice by fleeing into a neighbouring *Schaft*.

At the time of signing, it had been said that

the then Emperor, Tomas I, had been reluctant to endorse the article, but his hand had been forced by higher powers.

Regardless, the rule was Law, and there was nothing Dirk could do about it.

"We'll need a warrant," he said. "One that we can issue to the Guild in Kronnig."

Ing shook his head.

"It'd need to be signed..." he said.

"By whom?" Dirk asked.

"The Burgomeister," Ing replied glumly.

Dirk's heart sank in his chest.

He couldn't believe it.

He puffed out his cheeks in frustration then angrily slammed his hand against the filing shelf, sending a bundle of papers falling to the floor.

"Hey!" Ing yelled. "I just filed those!"

"Sorry," Dirk replied.

The Rhunligger gave him a mournful look.

"Maybe it'd be best if you let this one go?" he suggested.

"Accept defeat?" Dirk hissed. "But the man's a murderer..."

"Yes," the Rhunligger admitted. "But he's also powerful. He could destroy you if he wanted."

It was true.

Going after Klept was a dangerous game.

But it was nothing new to him.

In Ghis, he'd taken on Bakker, a murderous sergeant who'd massacred an entire village, and Araxys, the leader of the Elven Rebels.

The experienced had emboldened him.

"I'm not scared of him," Dirk said.

"Maybe you should be..." Ing laughed.

Dirk grinned and shook his head.

He then knelt down and started gathering up the documents that he'd knocked from the shelf.

As he started filing them away, he noticed that they were receipts for bounties.

Among them was the one they had collected earlier that day.

He remembered the doleful Clerk who'd issued it to them, a pedantic man who seemed obsessed with ensuring that every Schilling had been accounted for.

"When you're spending the Emperor's coin," the man had told them, *" every Dram must be logged... "*

Dirk's thoughts drifted to the *Schaftmoot*, and the exchange he'd witnessed between the Burgomeister and the man in the red chaperon.

"What happened to the money..." Dirk said aloud, echoing the man's words.

"Eh?" Ing responded.

"Receipts!" Dirk replied excitedly.

The Rhunligger looked at him as if he'd lost his mind.

"Yes," he remarked. "All around us. And they all need to be put away."

"No," Dirk said. "*Council* Receipts."

Ing appeared none the wiser.

"...For payments authorised by Klept," he explained. "The Clerk at the Courthouse told us that every Dram is logged. The man at the *Schaftmoot* said nothing had been spent. But we know for a fact that Klept didn't have the funds to pay for Mollat's field..."

" ...Despite increasing the Poll Tax," Ing finished.

"Exactly," Dirk said. "And if the reason he couldn't pay is because he blew the town funds, there'd be records of it at the town hall."

Ing smiled.

"Very clever," he said. "But you'll still need a warrant to conduct an audit."

Dirk looked him in the eye.

"Who said anything about a warrant?" he replied.

Ing shook his head.

"No," he growled. "Not again. I'm annoyed enough at having to do this for two weeks, let alone the rest of my working life..."

Dirk but his lip.

"I'm not asking you to come with me," he said.

"Good," Ing replied.

"...But I will need you to cover for me while I'm gone."

"How exactly?" Ing exclaimed.

"I don't know," Dirk said. "Be inventive.... Say I'm ill."

"Errol will check your bunk.," Ing replied.

"Not if you tell him it's River Fever," Dirk countered.

River Fever was a common ailment in the north of the Empire. Contracted from ingesting dirty water, the afflicted person experienced tremendous stomach cramps, which resulted in severe flatulence and diarrhoea. The smells produced were awful and lingered in the air for days.

"Fine," Ing said. "But if you get into trouble for this, don't expect me to speak in your defence when they haul your arse in front of a Judge."

"Don't worry," Dirk replied. "I'll tell them you nothing to do with it."

CHAPTER 6

After sneaking out of the Guildhouse, Dirk made his way down Flescher's Lane towards the town square.

It was getting dark, but thankfully the rain had now stopped falling, and the clouds had parted to reveal a Harvest Moon.

He turned onto the plaza and made his way toward the old theatre, where he climbed the steps and went inside.

A young woman was sitting behind a counter in the lobby.

She gave him a nervous look as he approached.

Dirk assumed it had something to do with his uniform. The dark grey tunic, braced with hardened leather, was quite imposing to look at, and often caused people to baulk.

"How can I help you?" she asked, the words tumbling from her mouth.

"I'm Guildsman Vanslow," Dirk declared confidently. "I'm here to inspect the town accounts."

"Oh," the woman replied, touching the silver chain at her throat. "Do you have an appointment?"

"Of course," Dirk lied.

She opened up a book that was sitting on the desk.

It was a diary, containing details of any expected visitors.

"I'm sorry," she said. "But I can't see your name on the list. Who are you here to see?"

Dirk looked at her and smiled.

But not with his eyes.

"Listen," he said. "I'm here to investigate a serious fraud. One which may implicate the entire council and all of its employees."

The woman visibly gulped.

"After I carry out my work, I'll be creating a list of subpoenas, starting with all the people involved in the cover up."

Her face turned white as snow.

"If you don't want your name on the list," Dirk continued, "I'd suggest you show me through."

"Of course," she said., her voice trembling.

She got up from her seat and made her way to the end of the desk, where she took a key from a rack on the wall.

She handed it to him and pointed to a corridor behind him.

"The records are kept in room nine," she said.

87

"Thanks," he replied, palming the key in his fist.

"What's the meaning of this?" a man called out behind him.

Dirk recognised the voice.

It belonged to Klept.

He turned to face him and saw that he was flanked on either side by two huge brutes, who appeared to be ex-servicemen.

"The Guild are here," the woman stated, somewhat obviously. "They've come to audit the accounts."

"Have they now?" Klept replied.

The Burgomeister looked Dirk in the eye, and a wave of recognition crossed his face.

"Ahh," he said. "It's you. You're back."

"I said I would be," Dirk replied.

"I hope you've come with a warrant this time?"

Dirk reached inside the lapel of his tunic, dropping the key into his inside pocket.

"Oh dear," he said, withdrawing his hand. "I appear to have misplaced it."

Klept cut his eyes at him.

"Or you never had it in the first place?" he replied.

Dirk smirked.

"Gentlemen," Klept said to his minders, "Please escort this man outside. He's overstayed his welcome."

"But I've just got here," Dirk remarked.

It was the wrong thing to say.

The two men stepped forward and each seized one of his arms. They then frogmarched him to the door and shunted him down the steps.

"This is the second time you've harassed me today," the Burgomeister shouted down at him from the top of the stairs. "If you trouble me a third time, I'll not treat you so politely."

Dirk grinned sarcastically then yanked his arms free.

He snorted and walked away.

* * *

Dirk stood in the shadows of the alleyway, watching the face of *Old Joe* as its hands creaked slowly towards the hour.

At eight o'clock, the bells inside the Town's tall Clocktower began to chime, scaring away a murder of rooks who were perched around the Belfry.

Dirk turned his gaze across the square to the Town Hall.

Before the bells stopped ringing, the twin doors opened and a crowd of workers spilled out of the building into the plaza, where they bade each other farewell before scurrying away to their homes.

Within minutes, the building was empty, and the doors were locked by the caretaker, who then made his way across the court towards *Boul-*

der's Avenue, which led to the bridge.

As soon as the man was out of sight, Dirk emerged from his hiding place and approached the wall surrounding the Town Hall's gardens.

It was eight feet tall and made from bricks that had been rendered with smooth plaster. Without a rope or a ladder, it would be impossible to climb.

He looked around for something he could stand on. In the shadows of a nearby snickelway, he saw the outline of a small dumpster. It was small, but big enough for big enough for his needs.

He jogged over and dragged it to a section of the wall that couldn't be seen from the main square. Shunting it up to the brickwork, he climbed upon its lid, then hauled himself up the wall and dropped down into the gardens on the other side.

As soon as his feet touched the ground, he dropped to his knees and hid behind a short hedge, which bordered the square lawn.

It was roughly forty yards long and featureless, save for a small fountain, which had been constructed at it centre.

Standing imperiously beyond it, were the walls of the Town Hall.

Dirk studied the building for a moment, looking for a way in.

Other than the rear door, which was made of oak and braced with iron cords, there were a number of windows set into the walls. The ones on the ground and first floors were nothing more than narrow slats, but on the second floor they were much larger, and all of them were fronted with wide balconies.

Dirk figured that if he could get himself up onto one of them, he could jimmy open a window and let himself inside.

To do this, however, he would need to get up onto the roof.

He quickly scanned the walls, and noticed a long leaden drainpipe running down from side of the building to the ground.

It looked sturdy enough to climb.

If he could get over to it without being seen, he could clamber up it to the gambrel, where he could drop down onto one of the balconies.

With his mind set, he got to his feet and started making his way across the lawn.

Suddenly, he heard the sound of footsteps.

He quickly ducked down behind the fountain, tucking in his arms and legs, so that he wouldn't be seen.

The footsteps got louder.

He peeked over the lip of the fountain's rim and saw two guards appear on the path. They were armed and wearing the livery of the town guard. Both of them looked bored and uninterested.

Dirk watched in silence as they made their way to the far end of the wall, before turning back on themselves.

He waited for them to disappear, then rose

to his feet and darted across the remainder of the lawn toward the drainpipe.

When he got there, the wrapped his hands around it and started to climb. The pipe was rigid and heavy, and made little sound as he ascended.

Moments later, he was up on the roof.

The moon hung wearily in the sky above him, its dim orange glow casting broken shadows behind the six chimneys that protruded from the rooftop.

Dirk crouched low and crossed the tarpaulin to the west side of the building. Once, there, he leant over the side and looked down at the balconies jutting out from the storey below.

The guards were nowhere in sight.

He crouched down and got onto his knees, then slowly began lowering himself over the side.

Taking hold of the ledge, he positioned himself directly above one of the balconies and allowed himself to drop.

He fell down through the air but landed awkwardly, twisting his ankle.

The pain caused him to yelp.

The guards must have heard him, for he heard their footsteps down below.

"What was that?" one of them said.

"Dunno..." said the other.

Dirk hugged the floor of the balustrade and pushed himself as far back as he could, to remain out of sight.

The guards didn't move.

They remained where they were on the path below, discussing what to do.

"We should go inside and check," the first one said.

"What if it's nothing?" the other man replied.

"Better to be safe than sorry..."

Dirk felt the blood draining from his face.

If they came inside and started looking, they'd surely find him.

And if that happened, he'd be taken back to the Guild, where he would then have to explain to Hamm what he was doing.

He couldn't let that happen.

He needed to distract them somehow.

He looked around.

Between the balustrade's palings was a small nest.

Inside it was a *Spire Rook,* a small black bird that made its home in the rooftops of buildings.

Its head emerged from its roost and it clucked at him angrily.

"Sorry," Dirk whispered, as he lifted his foot and poked the nest with his toe.

The *Spire Rook* cackled and pecked.

Dirk tapped the nest again, dislodging it from the rail.

The bird screeched then flapped its wings and flew off into the night.

"There you go," one of the guards say. "It was nothing... Just a bird."

The other man seemed satisfied, and the two

of them began walking away.

Dirk sighed.

When they were out of earshot, he got to his knees and drew the dagger from his belt.

Sliding the blade between the join of the window, he lifted the latch within. It squeaked then clicked open.

Taking hold of the pane to stop it moving, he ducked beneath the head jamb and slid his body through.

Once inside, he stood up to find himself in what appeared to be a storeroom. Boxes were stacked all around him. They contained old costumes and props, which were covered in dust.

The room looked unused, as if no one had been in it for years.

He quietly made his way over to the door and turned the handle.

It creaked open and he stepped outside.

He found himself in a narrow corridor with a series of doors either side.

He followed it to the right, where he came to the top of a staircase.

Looking down the steps, he saw nothing but darkness below.

He gingerly descended the stairs and came to a small landing, which was blocked by a door. He quietly opened it and looked outside.

It opened out into a wider corridor, which was lit with candles hanging from the walls. The passage stretched the entire breadth of the building.

He started walking down it and realised that it was the part of the second-floor concourse, which led to the upper seats of the gallery.

Halfway along, he came to the grand staircase, whose steps led down to the floors below.

He took hold of the rail and steadily made his way down, keeping an eye out for any of the night watchmen.

At the foot of the stairs, he found himself back in the lobby.

The twin chestnut doors stood in front of him.

To his right was the reception desk.

Remembering what the female clerk had told him earlier, he made his way down the corridor to his left and looked for a room number nine.

He found it at the far end.

It was guarded by a sturdy-looking door, which was braced with bands of iron.

He reached inside his pocket and pulled out the key.

He slid it inside the lock and gave it a turn.

The latch clicked and he pushed it open.

Inside, he found the room full of filing cabinets, which were set against all four walls.

Immediately, the enormity of his task hit him.

There was so much paper, so many files.

To find something here that would implicate Klept would be like looking for a needle in a haystack.

And nigh on impossible in the dark...

A large desk stood at the centre of the room.

Sitting upon it, was a lantern.

He made his over and lit the wick, using the scratch of flint that had been left beside it.

The flame flickered alive inside the glass cage, emitting a bright yellow light, which illuminated the room.

He left the lantern where it was and approached the blocks of files. To his relief, he saw that each one had been labelled.

He went over to the one which read, 'Invoices', and pulled out the drawer.

It was full of records.

Luckily, the papers had been filed in order, by year.

He lifted out the ones pertaining to 1216 and placed them on the desk, where he began studying them one-by-one on the table, squinting at the words in the dull glow of the moonlight.

A cursory look revealed nothing odd.

Most of the documents related to goods and services that had been procured by the council. Everything seemed to be in order, with dates, signatures, and official stamps.

However, towards the bottom of the pile, he found a strange receipt that had been made out to *Ruystin Fryk,* who was the owner of a company named, *Fryk's Chance.*

Dirk had heard of him.

He was a bookmaker on the eastern side of town.

The invoice struck him as odd.

An amount of twenty thousand Drams had been paid to Fryk, and it had been signed off by Klept.

Unlike the other invoices, however, it was missing the Imperial Stamp.

It certainly seemed odd.

Of all the payments made by the Council, why would one be made to a Bookie?

And why for so much?

Had Klept been gambling away the public's coin?

It would certainly explain why he didn't have the money to pay for Mollat's field.

Was this the evidence he'd been looking for?

Either way, it was suspicious and could not be ignored.

He decided to return to the Guild and present the document to Hamm.

Surely, once he saw it, it would be grounds enough to issue a warrant to question Klept, if not for murder then for corruption at least...

Then he turned toward the door, but before he could take a single step forward, he was struck on the side of the face with a heavy blunt rod.

The impact sent him spinning to the floor.

As he fell, his left temple connected with the edge of the tabletop.

Everything went black.

When Dirk came to, he found Klept standing over him.

The Burgomeister was holding the invoice in his hand.

"I had a feeling that one day this would come back to haunt me," he said, glancing at the document. "I made a mistake in assuming it'd never be found."

He smiled wistfully.

"No matter," he said. "Mistakes can be corrected..."

He stepped over to the table and held the paper above the lantern. It caught fire and started burning.

"Mistakes like Mollat?" Dirk said.

Klept sniggered.

"That mistake was his, not mine," he replied. "If the old fool hadn't been so stubborn to refuse my offer, he'd still be alive..."

Dirk smirked.

"He'd still be alive," he replied. "If you hadn't stolen the people's coin."

"I never stole anything," the Burgomeister snapped. "I merely borrowed it..."

"To place bets," Dirk finished.

Klept sneered at him.

"...I had every intention of returning what I'd taken," the Burgomeister replied. "But fortune conspired against me."

"So, what happened?" Dirk sniffed. "Did you horse come in last?"

Klept smiled resignedly.

"It wasn't horses," he replied, glancing at the paper burning in his hands. "It was the Durnborg Dodgers."

Dirk remembered reading about what had happened in the final of Emperor's Cup. The Dodgers' had controlled the game from start to finish but were beaten by a last-minute Drop Goal that had been scored from the centre line. It had been a shock result, no one had expected it.

"If they'd have won that game, I would have made enough coin to scrap the hated Poll Tax..."

"So, now you're a philanthropist...?" Dirk mocked.

"I'm a realist," Klept replied, dropping what was left of the document into the lantern. "My popularity wanes," he continued, "while the *Scarlet Faction's* grows. I feared that come the Spring, they'd have the numbers to oust me. But scrapping the Citizen's Standard would have changed everything."

He lifted the lantern from the table.

Its light cast an eerie glow over his features.

"But now my all hopes rest on the *Erntfest*. If it goes well, the people will remember it when they cast their ballots."

Dirk smirked.

"So Mollat was killed to save your job..."

"Mollat was killed to save this *town*," Klept sneered. "If those *Anarchists* took charge, Durnborg would be plunged into chaos."

"Maybe that's what the people want?"

The Burgomeister sniffed and shook his head.

"People want stability, order, and peace," he replied. "They may think they want change but if they ever got it, they'd soon be pining for the way things were."

He stepped forward and began tipping over the cabinets.

Dirk watched from knees as a mountain of documents spilled across the floor.

"You can't dress this up as a burglary," Dirk mocked. "I saw the invoice. I can question Fryk."

Klept laughed.

"You won't be questioning anyone," he rasped.

He threw the lantern at the fallen papers. The glass burst on impact and the burning oil inside spattered the documents, instantly setting them alight.

Dirk got to his feet as the fire quickly took hold.

Within a few seconds, it raged fiercely, blocking his route to the door.

"I told you I wouldn't be so polite if our paths crossed a third time," Klept laughed, smiling at him through the flames. "Consider this a promise kept."

He turned and left the room.

Dirk stepped back.

The fire was spreading quickly.

With each second that passed, another stack burst into flames.

He looked around for a means of escape.

A series of windows were set high into the walls, but they were too small to squeeze through and had been barred with iron grates.

The door was the only way out.

But to get to it, he would have to risk jumping through the fire.

He steeled himself and moved forward.

If he could run through fast enough, there was chance the flames might not burn him.

Just then, the cabinet next to the doorway exploded from the heat, and its stricken shell crumbled onto its side, blocking the exit.

There was no way out.

Smoke began to fill the room.

Dirk coughed and covered his mouth with his hand.

If he didn't get out soon, he'd choke to death.

He retreated from the flames.

The air was getting hot.

He started to panic.

The suddenly, he felt a draft of cool air.

Glancing in its direction, he saw that it was coming from a fireplace that stood against the far wall.

He quickly rushed over and crouched beside

it.

He ducked beneath the grate and looked up into the chimney stack.

Above him, he saw the glow of the moonlight reflecting off the top of the flue.

It was a way out.

He shifted his body into the hearth then pressed his hands against the sides of the wall.

He did the same with his feet and began shimmying himself upwards.

A plume of smoke rose up through the hearth beneath him, billowing up over his legs and body.

He coughed as he inhaled the burning air, then continued to climb, slowly working his way up.

He became aware of a light below him.

The flames had reached the grate.

The fire roared and the smoke became more intense.

He held his breath and closed his eyes.

The air was getting hotter.

If he didn't reach the top fast, he'd be broiled alive.

Suddenly, his hands touched the crown of the stack.

He'd reached the top.

The only thing barring his way was the chimney cap, which topped the flue.

He braced his legs against the sides of the stack and punched his arms upwards.

The cap creaked under the force of his blow

but didn't break.

He hit it again.

On the third strike, it broke away from its rivets, pinging across the roof.

Dirk hauled himself up and swung his body over the lip.

He dropped down onto the surface of the flat roof, where he immediately he started coughing,

After he'd finally caught his breath, he crawled to the edge of the rooftop towards the leaden drainpipe.

Once there, he took hold of the guttering, and swung his legs over the side and began shimmying himself down.

During his descent, he heard the fires raging within the building's interior.

The flames had spread quickly.

It would soon become engulfed.

As he passed by the third-floor window, it shattered, and shards of glass rained down onto the lawn below. A thick plume of smoke then billowed from the hole.

Above the noise of the raging flames, he heard the sound of screaming on the street below.

He turned his head towards the sound and saw that a large crowd had formed within the town square. They were watching the Hall as it burned, many of them shaking their heads in disbelief.

A bell started ringing in the distance, and a troop of the Town Guard appeared carrying buckets. The crowd parted to let them through, and the men formed a line between the building and the fountain. The buckets were dipped into the pool and passed through their hands to the man at the front, who cast the water inside onto the flames.

But it was pointless.

The fire was raging too hard.

There was no hope of putting it out.

Dirk reached the bottom of the pipe and planted his feet on the floor.

He looked up at the smoke billowing through the shattered windows.

The whole building would soon be raised to the ground, along with everything inside...

Still, his endeavour had not been a total loss.

Despite the loss of the invoice, he could still approach the bookie and question him about the Burgomeister's wager. The man would surely have a receipt of the bet, which he could then show to Hamm.

With any luck, it would be enough to convince the Guildcaptain to reopen the case and issue a warrant for Klept's arrest.

But to get to the bookie, he would need to escape the garden without being seen...

He turned and made his way over to the wall, but within a few steps, he was ordered to stop by the two guards who had been patrolling the grounds.

"You!" one of them yelled. "Stop where you are!"

"Halt!" screamed the other.

Dirk dashed toward the wall.

He couldn't allow himself to be caught.

He raced over the lawn and vaulted the hedgerow.

The guards chased after him.

He built up speed as he approached the wall then jumped up with arms raised.

His fingertips touched the ledge but couldn't find purchase on the smooth plasterwork.

He slid down to the ground.

Glancing over his shoulder, he saw the guards closing in.

He turned and jumped again, but without any speed to lift him higher, his hands fell short of the lip.

"Grab him," one of the of guards said.

A gauntleted hand seized his shoulder.

Dirk turned and faced them both, raising his arms in submission.

His action was met with a punch to the face.

The blow forced him backwards into the wall, winding him.

Before he could regain his composure, the men were either side of him.

They seized his arms and began frogmarching him away.

* * *

Dirk was shunted through a side gate and

brought to the front of the building, where he was presented to the men of the Town Guard. The sergeant stepped out of the bucket line and came up to them.

"We found man inside the grounds," one of the guards said.

"He was trying to escape through the garden," his comrade added.

"Fleeing the scene of the crime, eh?" the Sergeant snarled, as he wiped a pall of soot from his forehead.

"I'm no arsonist," Dirk replied. "Look at me. Can't you see I'm a Guildsman."

He gestured to the Iron Seal on his lapel.

The officer hummed.

"Release him," he said.

The guards looked shocked.

"But, Sir," one said, "We caught him red-handed!"

"Take him back to the Guildhouse," the Sergeant replied. "Tell his Captain what you saw."

"No," a voice shouted.

Dirk glanced to his left and saw Klept emerging from the crowd.

"You will arrest this man at once," he said. "He's an errant rogue, working for himself. My men found him trying to the enter the Hall earlier without a warrant. I suspected he was up to no good... It seems I've been proven right."

The sergeant tuned to Dirk.

"Do you have good reason to be here?" he

asked.

Without a warrant to protect him, Dirk could offer no defence.

"I'm investigating a murder," was all he could muster.

"That wasn't the question," the Sergeant replied.

Dirk fell silent.

The officer snorted.

"Put him in chains and take him to the Courthouse," he ordered. "Have him charged with arson."

"I'm innocent," Dirk protested.

"Save it for the Judge," the man replied.

The guards bound his hands the started leading him away through the crowd.

Many of the townsfolk appeared shocked at what they were seeing. For most, it had been the first time they'd ever seen a Guildsman in chains.

The same could be said for a group of his comrades, gathered at the edge of the square, who'd left their drinks at *The Glass* to see what was going on.

They looked at him with sour expressions.

"It's not what it looks like," Dirk pleaded.

Guildcaptain Hamm pushed his way to the front of the throng.

"What's the meaning of this?" he asked, haughtily.

"What does it look like?" one of the soldiers replied. "This miscreant set fire to the Town Hall.

We're taking him to the Gaol."

"No, you're not," the Guildcaptain replied. "Guildsmen are tried separately from other citizens. We have our own Courts and Laws."

The Guardsmen laughed.

"If you have a problem," the man replied. "Take it up with the Burgomeister."

The indignation disappeared from Hamm's face.

He stepped back, allowing the men to pass.

"Hamm!" Dirk called, as he was shunted on.

The Guildcaptain averted his eyes.

Dirk looked to the rest of the group for aid, but no one lifted a finger to help him.

He couldn't blame them.

The optics were terrible.

From their point of view, all they were seeing was one of their own being led in cuffs.

He'd shamed his Vows.

He'd shamed the Guild.

He'd shamed them.

What the guardsman said had been right.

The only person who'd listen to him now was the Judge...

CHAPTER 7

The guards ushered Dirk through the doors of the Courthouse and shunted him toward the counter.

The same Clerk who had been on duty that morning was sitting behind it. The man ignored them as they approached, refusing to take his eyes off the scroll that had been laid out on the desk in front of him.

After waiting patiently for several moments, one of the guards coughed to get his attention.

The Clerk raised his free hand and extended his index finger.

"Wait," the man said.

The militiamen didn't know how to respond.

"Excuse me, Sir," one of them said. "We have a prisoner."

The Clerk pursed his lips.

"The Guildsman will do the talking," he said.

The guards looked at each other before the other one answered.

109

"But *he's* the prisoner..."

The Clerk immediately stopped writing.

He placed down the quill and raised his head.

The man looked Dirk up and down, and his eyes came to rest on the Iron Seal that was sewn in the left lapel of this tunic.

The Clerk shook his head dismissively.

"How the mighty do fall," he muttered.

His eyes turned to the guards.

"What's the charge?" he asked.

"Arson," the first Guard replied. "He burned down the Town Hall."

The Clerk tutted then pulled a book from behind the counter and opened it out on the table. He picked up his quill and started writing something on the page.

"What is the accused's name?"

The Guards didn't know.

They hadn't asked.

"Guildsman Vanslow," Dirk replied, sparing them their blushes.

"And your forename?"

"Dirk."

The Clerk snorted through his nostrils.

"Is that short for anything?" he asked.

"No," Dirk replied.

"Very well."

The Clerk wrote more words on the page. He took his time, as he had done that morning.

When he'd finally finished, he rang the bell on his desk and two gaolers appeared from the corridor leading to the cells.

"Cell five, please," he said.

The men came forward and took him from the guards.

They wheeled him round and took him through the corridor to the Gaoler's Office, where his weapons were placed inside a heavy oaken chest.

They then led him down a staircase to a dimly lit cell block.

There were ten cages in all.

Each of them was numbered.

The guards led him to the one labelled 'five' then shunted him inside, slamming the door behind him.

The room was plunged into darkness.

Dirk began shuffling forward, and as his eyes adjusted to the light, he made out the shape of a bench in front of him.

It was set against the wall beneath a grated window, and a man was sleeping upon it.

The figure stirred in the darkness.

"Who's that?" the man asked, sitting up on his bunk.

Dirk stepped forward into the sliver of moonlight that shone through the window.

"I'm Dirk," he said.

The man leaned forward and peered at his face.

"I know you," he said.

He got to his feet, and as he came forward

into the light, Dirk recognised him as the man he'd arrested earlier that day.

"Yossell?" he said. "You remember me?"

The man returned a crooked smile.

"How can I forget the man who took away my liberty?" he answered.

"I was only doing my job," Dirk responded, backing away.

"Quite diligently, as I recall..." Yossell replied. "I was on the bridge, yards away from freedom, yet you chose to pursue me regardless."

"What would you have me do?" Dirk responded. "Let you go?"

The man sniffed.

"Would it have made any difference if you had?" he remarked. "You were hardly taking a dangerous criminal off the streets?"

"You're a tax dodger," Dirk replied.

"It's an unfair tax," Yossell spat.

It was hard to disagree.

But Dirk wasn't in the mood for politics.

"You broke the law," he said.

Yossell laughed.

"Look who's talking..."

The hypocrisy of his position was self-evident.

Yet despite the optics, there was a difference.

He was innocent.

"So, what did you do to find yourself in here?" the man asked. "Did you threaten a warrant? Beat a suspect?"

The suggestion offended him.

"I did no such thing," Dirk snapped.

"Then what did you do?"

Dirk leant up against the wall and folded his arms..

"I went after the wrong man," he said, grimly.

Yossell smirked.

"An innocent man?"

Dirk looked him in the eye.

"No," he replied. "He was guilty."

"What of?" Yossel pressed. "Breathing?"

"Murder," Dirk replied.

The man's face dropped.

"Murder? In Durnborg?" he exclaimed. "Who was killed?"

"Kurgen Mollat," Dirk replied.

"That old miser? Yossell hissed, shaking his head. "Well, I suppose the world's a better place without him."

"His killer said pretty much the same thing," Dirk remarked.

Yossell curled his lip.

"Your man admitted it?"

Dirk nodded.

Yossell looked confused.

"So why didn't you bring him in?"

"I tried," Dirk admitted. "But he outsmarted me. Then he framed me for something I didn't do."

Yossell gave him an incredulous look.

"How did he manage that?"

Dirk sighed.

"He's a man of power and influence," he replied.

"Who is he?" Yossell pressed.

"You'd wouldn't believe me if I told you," Dirk remarked.

"Try me," his cellmate replied.

Dirk clicked his tongue.

"Ok," he said. "It was the Kohn Klept."

"The Burgomeister?" Yossell exclaimed.

Dirk nodded.

The man gritted his teeth.

"I've always known the man to be villain," he said, "but murder is a new low... Even for him."

He paced over to the window and looked out through bars.

"When my comrades hear of this, it'll be the end of him, for sure."

"Your comrades?" Dirk said.

"Aye," Yossell replied. "The *Scarlet Faction*."

Dirk chuckled.

"Well good luck in getting the word out to them," he smirked. "By the time they let you go, the election would have been and gone..."

Yossell smiled devilishly.

"I wouldn't be so sure about that," he quipped.

Dirk gave him a curious look.

"What do you mean?" he asked.

"My friends are breaking me out of here," Yossell replied, with a smile.

"When?" Dirk asked.

"Tonight," the man replied, gesturing to the window. "Just after midnight. It's all been arranged."

Dirk stood up.

"You have to take me with you," he said.

Yossell sniffed.

"Why?" he asked.

"I need to be out there," Dirk replied, "...so I can bring Klept to justice."

The man laughed.

"How's that worked out for you so far?"

"Please," Dirk implored. "There's people I need to speak to, evidence I need to collect... I can build a case against Klept, believe me.

"You've had your chance, Guildsman," Yossell replied. "But I fear more permanent solution is required to mend this town's corruption."

"What do you mean?" Dirk asked.

The man smiled.

"A revolution," he replied. "The time is ripe for it and this incident will be the catalyst."

Dirk baulked at the suggestion.

"Do you honestly believe the people will rise?"

"Of course," he replied, "For too long, the people of Durnborg have been blind to the lies they've been fed by their rulers. When they're finally presented with the truth, I've no doubt they'll cast off their chains and join us."

There was a sincerity to his words.

It was clear he believed everything he was

saying.

There was truth in it too, for if Yossell and his men could muster even a tenth of the population to their cause, both the Guard and the Guild would be overrun.

But Dirk couldn't help but doubt whether the docile people of the town had it in themselves to be Rebels.

From his experience in Gefghed, he knew it took a certain mindset.

It was one thing to grumble about the Emperor, but another thing entirely to take up arms and march against him.

It required courage and grit.

Two qualities that were scarcely present in the local population.

"Let's say the people do rise," Dirk said, hypothetically. "What then?"

"Then others will join us," Yossell replied, excitedly. "Our actions here will ignite a fuse, one that will quickly spread to the four corners of the nation."

His eyes glazed over, dreamily.

"Within months," he continued, "the Emperor will fall, and the people will finally be free of his yolk."

It was wishful, idealistic thinking.

Yossell was a romantic.

Just like Marfine.

He suddenly had an idea.

"I've heard this sort of talk before," Dirk said.

"Where?" Yossell asked.

"Gefghed," Dirk replied. "When I ran with the *Swords of Sheenah*."

Yossell laughed at him through his nose.

"Come again?" he replied. "Maybe it's the absence of light in here, but if I'm not mistaken, you're wearing the symbol of their sworn enemy..."

He gestured to the Iron Seal on Dirk's chest.

"If we're talking symbols," he replied, "what do you think of this?"

Dirk slid his hand beneath the cut of his lapel and pulled out his copy of the *She'En.*

"Where did you get that?" Yossell asked.

"From a friend of mine," Dirk answered. "You may have heard of her? Marfine Delefries."

Yossell's eyes widened.

"The Elven Rebel?"

Dirk nodded.

"How do you know her?" Yossell asked.

"I helped her during my time in the colonies." The man shook his head.

"But you're a Guildsman?" he said.

"That didn't stop me saving her life," Dirk replied. "And she did the same for me in Einhof."

Yossell's mouth opened.

"You're Dirk Vanslow," he said. "I read about your trial. You spoke out against the Emperor."

Dirk nodded.

"I may have said the words," he admitted, "But they were never printed."

Following his trial, Dirk had read the article

that had been written about him in the *Imperial Post*. The scribe who'd interviewed him had deliberately omitted everything he'd said about the war.

"They were," Yossell replied. "...In, *The Peasant's Voice*."

It was an underground publication, used by the *Scarlet Faction* to spread their message.

Copies of the magazine were banned from sale, but it was easy enough to get your hands on a copy if you knew where to look.

"You're a hero to our cause!"

Dirk shrugged his shoulders.

"You must join us," Yossell said, excitedly. "With someone like you at our head, the Revolution we'll be unstoppable!"

"I'd be happy to help," Dirk lied. "But first you'll need to get me out of here..."

* * *

Dirk heard the tolling of the bell tower in the Square.

The chimes were dull and hollow, numbering twelve in all.

Yossell was stood on the bunk, peering through the bars of the small window above the bed.

It looked out over *Durn's Park*, which stood between the town's centre and its poorer, Eastern District. The daub and timber tenements of *The*

Wash rose up high beyond the distant treeline, their ugly brown roofs glistening dully beneath the moon's orange glow.

Yossell snorted through his nose.

"Where are they?" he muttered.

He was getting impatient.

"They should be here by now...."

"Don't panic," Dirk replied. "It's only just turned Midnight."

As if on cue, a horse whinnied outside.

Yossell turned from the bed.

"It's them!" he beamed.

Dirk put his head to the grate and saw a cart pulling up on the street outside. Two figures climbed down from its bench and one of them came over to the window.

He crouched down as he approached the wall.

"Nye?" he called.

"Erik!" Yossell replied. "Here!"

The man came up to the bars of their cell.

Yossell reached through the grate and shook the man's hand.

"I thought you'd abandoned me," he said.

"Never, Comrade," the man replied with a grin.

He then jogged back to the cart and lifted a length of chain from its bed. Attached to its end was a grapple.

The man ran back to them and hooked it around the grate.

He stood up and waved to the driver, who gave the man a nod and lashed his reins over the backs of the horses.

The steeds snorted and moved forward.

Dirk watched the chain begin to unwind, drawing tighter as the cart moved further away.

Moments later, it was completely stretched out, and began shaking under the strain.

The grate creaked as it struggled to keep its hold on the wall.

Then, with a loud ping, suddenly sprang free, landing on the street with a dull clunk.

Erik ran to the opening and reached his hand inside.

Yossell took it.

"There's someone else in here who's coming with us," he said.

His comrade nodded then pulled him up through the gap.

The two men then reached in and Dirk took their hands.

With a mighty heave, he lifted him out of the cell onto the cobblestones of the street.

Dirk glanced up at the sky.

He'd never felt so relieved to be free.

"Quickly," Erik said to them. "Get to the horses. It won't take the guards long to work out what's happened."

They rushed to the front of the cart.

The driver had already abandoned his seat and was climbing up into the saddle of the horse on the left.

He reached out his hand to Erik, who took him by the wrist. With a sharp yank, he hauled his comrade up onto the seat behind him.

Yossell ran over to the second horse.

But Dirk was quicker.

In a flash, he booted the stirrup and sprung up onto the horse's back.

He took the reins then glanced over his shoulder.

Yossell was a yard or so behind him.

He extended his hand, willing Dirk to take it.

But instead, the Guildsman offered the heel of his boot.

The kick was gentle, but enough to knock the man off his feet, and he landed on his back with a thump.

The men on the other horse looked over at him.

At first, they weren't sure whether Dirk's actions had been intentional or an accident.

He answered them with a single word.

"Sorry."

He then dugs his heels into the horse's side and spurred it into a gallop through the park.

Yossell's companions were angry.

They started cursing him, as they chased him across the field.

With nothing to see by but the light of the moon, Dirk headed for the glowing tenements that lay beyond the treeline.

"Traitor!" one of the men shouted.

"Scum!" yelled the other.

Their words were soaked with bile.

They wanted to kill him for what he had done.

But Dirk had greater concerns to trouble him.

Up ahead was a stream.

It crossed the path in front of him.

There was no bridge.

He'd have to jump across.

There was no time to think.

He lashed his horse's reins, and it thundered towards the water's edge.

With a mighty roar, Dirk urged it to jump.

The stallion snorted then launched itself up into the air.

Time seemed to stand still as it sailed over the gap, before crashing down onto the other side, without so much as breaking its stride.

Dirk glanced back at his pursuers.

Their horse had come to a stop near the water's edge.

The two men on its back were waving their fists at him, screaming bloody murder.

Dirk allowed himself a wry smile.

He'd escaped...

CHAPTER 8

Once he'd reached the other side of the park, Dirk climbed down from the stallion's saddle and patted it on the nose.

The horse looked happy.

Dirk imagined it had enjoyed the night's excitement.

It certainly beat pulling carts...

He tapped it on the rump and sent it darting off into the park.

Someone would find it the next morning.

He hoped it would be Yossell.

The park was separated from the eastern quarter by a wrought iron fence. He followed it south until he came to a gate, then slipped through quietly after checking no one was around.

He knew that it wouldn't long before the alarm was raised at the Gaol. Once the Court learned of his escape, an alert would be sent to the town guard, and they would send out patrols to find him. If he'd not been found by morning, a warrant would be issued and sent to the Guild.

The prospect of being hunted by his brothers scared him.

He knew they'd stop at nothing to bring him in.

It was a matter of honour and pride.

But hopefully, it wouldn't come to that.

If all went well, he'd return to the Guild before dawn, in possession of evidence that both vindicated him and implicated Klept in Mollat's murder.

But it all rested on finding Ruystin Fryk...

Lifting up his collar, Dirk made his way across the cobbled road and through the snickel-way that separated two giant tenements.

Sticking to the shadows, he worked his way east in pursuit of the bookmaker.

* * *

Fryk's Chance stood on the corner of Cobbler's row, a commercial area of the Eastern District, which housed a number of shops and businesses. Most of them were squalid and poor, selling nothing more than worthless trinkets, second-hand tat, and hand-me-down clothes that had been donated by the town's wealthier denizens. Their frontages were cracked and chipped, the signs hanging above their shops where old and poorly stencilled, and uncollected rubbish littered the pavement outside their doors.

A VOW OF SUCCOUR

Dirk wondered how much money one could earn running businesses such as these.

Surely not enough to make a decent living...

But then again, that was true of everyone who lived in *The Wash*.

Well, nearly everyone.

Fryk appeared to be doing well.

Amongst the decay, his Gambling Hall was a picture of opulence.

It had been designed in the style of an ancient temple, similar in appearance to the Town Hall, with marble pillars and a flat-topped roof.

Above its double doors was a bold sign, which read 'Fryk's Chance'. It stencilled in the font of Old Prutch but its garish colour made it appear chintzy.

Standing in front of the doors was an Ogre.

Dirk had seen him before.

He'd been in Klept's dressing room after the *Schaftmoot*.

A Dwarf had been with him at the time.

Had this been Fryk?

He climbed the steps of the Gambling Hall and approached the doors.

The Ogre glared at his uniform suspiciously.

"Go away," he growled. "We're shut."

Dirk stood and listened at the door.

He heard a rumbling of people inside.

"Doesn't sound shut to me," he replied.

"We're shut to the likes of you," the beast roared.

"Why? Dirk replied. "Because I'm a Guildsman?"

The Ogre nodded.

"No lawmen," he said. "It makes our customers nervous."

Dirk smiled.

"They've nothing to fear from me," he said. "I'm here to see Fryk."

The brute glared at him.

"Master Fryk sees no one," he growled.

"He'll see me," Dirk replied. "It's about Klept."

The Ogre's lips trembled.

Dirk wasn't sure if he was enraged or merely taking his time processing his words.

"Come with me," he said finally.

The beast pushed open the doors and gestured for him to enter.

Dirk stepped inside and found himself in a large hall.

It was dimly lit, and the air was filled with scented smoke.

Dirk cast his eyes around the room.

Directly ahead, at the bottom of a short staircase, was a gaming pit. It was surrounded on all sides by a wooden gallery containing nests of tables, where people were sitting drinking and playing cards.

Some of them were leaning over the rail, watching the game of *Pinfinger* that was being played on the arena floor.

A large crowd were gathered around the two

participants. They were cheering and placing bets. A group of scantily clad girls were mingling among them, serving them drinks and planting small kisses on their cheeks.

The whole place reeked of debauchery.

"Follow me," the Ogre growled.

He led him through the gallery to an office at the back of the room.

It had large windows that overlooked the pit.

The glass of each one was protected by a set of oaken slats, which prevented anyone on the floor from seeing inside.

The Ogre stopped outside the door.

"Wait," he said, lifting up his hand and pressing it against Dirk's chest.

Dirk did as he was told.

The brute knocked on the door and waited.

Moments later, Dirk heard its latch click and it opened to reveal the face of a Dwarf.

"Master Fryk," the Ogre said. "You have a visitor."

He moved aside and pointed at Dirk.

"You stupid lug!" the Dwarf retorted. "I thought I told you I wasn't to be disturbed."

"Sorry master," the Ogre mumbled. "But he says it's about Klept."

Fryk blew out his cheeks.

"Fine," he said. "Wait here. I'll be out shortly."

He closed the door and disappeared inside.

Dirk heard the Dwarf shouting within.

Seconds later the door opened and young

woman came out. She was half naked, carrying her clothes in her hands.

When she saw Dirk, her cheeks blushed.

She smiled nervously then gave him a little curtsey before rushing off down the gallery.

Fryk then reappeared at the door.

"Ok," he said. "Come in."

He opened up the door and gestured for them to enter.

The Ogre stepped back and allowed Dirk to pass, then followed him into the office.

The Dwarf locked the door behind him.

"So," he began as he approached the large desk, which faced the window. "What's this about?"

He picked up a goblet, which was sitting on the table, then began filling it with wine from a flagon.

"Kurgen Mollat," Dirk replied. "I'm investigating his murder."

The Dwarf sniffed.

"I thought you said this was about Klept?"

"It is," Dirk said.

Fryk smiled wickedly.

"I never thought he had it in him..."

He took a swig from the glass.

"So why is it you're speaking to me?" Fryk asked. "Shouldn't you be out there looking for him?"

"I need evidence," Dirk replied, "...the receipts for his betting slips."

The Dwarf guffawed into his goblet.

"Is he having a laugh?" he chuckled, looking at the Ogre.

"I'm being serious," Dirk replied.

"So am I" Fryk said. "My customers are important to me. And so is their privacy."

"A man's been murdered," Dirk said.

"So?" the Dwarf replied. "Men get murdered all the time."

"Not in Durnborg."

Fryk swished the wine around the circle of his glass.

"It may come as a surprise to you," he began, his voice tinged with sarcasm, "but gambling isn't considered a noble pursuit."

He placed the glass on the table.

"If word got out that I was a man who handed over the names of his clientele to anyone who came asking, I'd soon find my hall empty."

He glanced at the Ogre.

"...And how then would I be able to pay Klug's wages?"

The brute frowned and nodded.

"If I come back with a warrant, you'll have to hand them over," Dirk warned.

Fryk grinned devilishly.

"I don't think you will," he said.

"Why not?" Dirk replied.

The Dwarf studied him with his eyes.

"Where's your sword?" he asked.

Dirk's hand unconsciously drifted to his

empty scabbard.

"I left it behind," he said.

"When you knew you were coming to a place like this?" Fryk laughed. "Pull the other one."

He took a step forward.

"What?" Dirk stuttered. "You don't believe me?"

"I'll tell you what I believe..." Fryk replied.

Dirk stepped back.

"...I believe you're the Guildsman who escaped from the county Gaol tonight. The same one who's wanted by the Guard for burning down the Town Hall."

Dirk smiled nervously.

"Why do you say that?" he asked.

"I have eyes and ears everywhere in this town," Fryk replied. "There aint nothing that happens without me knowing it..."

Dirk took another step back.

He bumped into the Ogre, who was standing behind him.

"I also know there's a pretty reward for anyone who brings you in."

He gave a nod to Klug and the beast seized Dirk's arms, pinning them to his sides.

"You're making a mistake," Dirk warned. "Klept's tying up his loose ends. If you don't help me, he'll be coming for you next."

Fryk laughed.

"Let him come," he replied. "I'm not scared of him... This is Klept we're talking about.... not Ruul-bloody-Zamar!"

He gestured for the Ogre to take him outside and the brute turned him towards the door.

The situation was looking dire.

If he was returned to the Town Guard, it was likely he'd spend the rest of his life behind bars.

He had to do something.

And quickly.

Thinking fast, he raised his boot and brought his heel down hard upon the Ogre's instep.

The beast howled and released his arms.

Seizing his opportunity, Dirk ran to the door and pulled at the handle.

It didn't budge.

"Looking for this?" Fryk said.

Dirk turned and saw that he was holding up the key.

"Get him Klug," the Dwarf ordered. "And this time, don't be so gentle with him..."

The Ogre grinned.

He punched his fist into his palm then came forward.

Dirk waited for him to raise his arms, then ducked beneath his armpit and dashed across the room.

The Dwarf hissed with frustration.

"Stop messing around Klug! Get him!"

The Ogre turned and marched towards him.

He looked furious.

Dirk knew there was no way he could beat the monster in a fist fight, so quickly scanned the room for something he could use as a weapon.

The only thing to hand was the wooden chair, sitting behind Fryk's desk.

He picked up and swung it at the brute.

The Ogre put out his hand and seized it in mid-air.

He smiled a toothy grin.

Dirk panicked.

He let go of the chair and dashed over to the table.

The Dwarf then came at him from the other side.

Dirk rolled backwards onto the tabletop, flicking out his leg.

His boot struck Fryk on the nose.

He stumbled backwards, his face streaming with blood.

"Bastard!" he cried. "You broke my nose!"

The Ogre glanced at his master, then turned his eyes to Dirk.

His fat head dripped with sweat.

The beast roared and stepped forward.

He lifted the chair above his head and brought it down.

Dirk could do nothing more than leap out of the way.

As he hit the floor, he heard a mighty crash behind him.

Looking up, he saw the Ogre at the window, struggling to entangle the legs of the chair, which had been caught within the slats.

A VOW OF SUCCOUR

With an angry grunt, he ripped it free, but in the process left a huge hole in the fenestra.

Dirk didn't need time to think.

He scrambled to his feet then threw himself through the gap, landing on the Pinfinger table below.

The crowd roared in shock and horror.

Dirk glanced up at the players.

Both were holding daggers.

One of them was missing a finger.

The audience fell silent and looked to the referee...

...Who responded by awarding the match to the other player.

The crowd went berserk.

People started yelling at each other, spitting and throwing glasses.

Within seconds the entire pit erupted into a mass brawl.

Dirk rolled off the table and looked up to the gallery.

Fryk and Klug were coming out of the office and making their way over to the stairs.

Dirk got to his feet and began running for the exit, but people were blocking his way.

He felt someone grab his shoulder.

He glanced back to see it was the player who'd lost his finger.

The man was enraged and slashed at Dirk's face with his dagger, he jumped back and avoided the blade.

The fingerless man spat and came at him, but his route was blocked by another man, who was pushed between them.

Dirk span on his heels and ran for the door...

...But the stairway was now blocked by the Dwarf's manservant.

"Look what he's done!" Fryk raged. "He's wrecked the whole joint!"

He looked at Dirk with fury in his eyes.

"Kill him!" he rasped.

The Ogre came down the steps and marched towards him, swatting aside anyone who got in his way.

Dirk backed up.

He felt a shunt in his back.

He turned and saw the Pinfinger player behind him, dagger in hand.

He drove the blade toward Dirk's throat.

Remembering his training, Dirk twisted into the strike and then barred the man's wrist with his hands. He then used the momentum of the thrust to guide the blade into the chest of the Ogre standing behind him.

Its point pierced the slab of meat above the brute's nipple and he screamed like a small girl.

Dirk released the Pinfinger Player's arm and stepped back.

The Ogre removed the dagger from his chest and grabbed the man by the collar.

"It wasn't my fault!" he whimpered, pointing at Dirk.

But Klug wasn't in the mood to listen.

He picked him up off the floor and began butting him with his monstrously oversized skull.

Dirk seized the moment.

He made a dash for the stairs.

Fryk was waiting at the top.

His arms were outstretched to block his path.

Dirk dipped his head and ran straight into him, knocking the Dwarf on his back.

"I'll get you for this," he heard Fryk yell behind him, as he crashed through the doors and escaped into the night...

CHAPTER 9

Dirk waited for the patrol to pass.

From the darkness of the alleyway, he watched the five militiamen make their way up the street before turning the corner.

They were out in force, looking for him.

It would only be a matter of time before he was found.

Dirk assessed his situation.

Turning himself in was not an option.

Neither was seeking solace from the Guild.

Without the evidence to vindicate himself, doing both would see him charged, tried and possibly hanged.

His only option now was to escape.

Then he could regroup and figure out what to do.

Leaving through the town gates would be risky. By now they would all be locked and guarded. The County Bridge would also be closed.

It left him with no choice but to escape by

river.

But to do that, he'd need to make his way to the west of town then find a boat to take him out.

At this time of night, it would tricky.

The Durnborg Dock was closed to shipping after sundown. It was guarded at night by a troop of customs officers, who patrolled the Harbour.

Dirk would have to evade detection, steal a boat, then sail it out of town without being seen.

It was a tall order.

But he had no choice.

He steeled himself and left the shadows, darting across the street into the park. He then made his way south through the trees before turning west, where he crossed the stream using the footbridge.

Once he was on the other side, he continued forwards, heading in the direction of the town centre.

At the edge of the park, he hid behind a hedge and looked out onto the street.

Militiamen were everywhere.

As soon as he stepped out, he would be seen.

He waited for a while to see if they would move on, but they remained where they were.

He grunted in frustration.

He needed to get past them somehow.

A distraction, maybe?

But what?

Nothing seemed to come to mind.

He needed a miracle.

Help me Sheenah, he whispered under his breath. *I need you now.*

He suddenly felt a hand touch him on the shoulder.

He spun round and aimed at punch at the figure, who caught his fist in the air, and put him in an armlock.

Seconds later, he was on the ground, immobilised.

It's over, he thought. *They'd caught him...*

He glanced up at his captor and saw a familiar pair of eyes staring back.

"Ing?"

"Yes, you idiot, it's me," the Rhunligger whispered.

He released Dirk's arm.

"Sorry," Dirk replied. "I thought you were one of them."

"Thank V'Loire I wasn't..." Ing chuckled.

"What are you doing here?" he asked.

"I heard about the Jailbreak," his friend said. "So, I thought I'd come looking for you."

"There's a warrant for me already?" Dirk gasped.

"No," Ing replied. "...But it's being written as we speak."

"You could get into a lot of trouble for helping me," Dirk warned.

"I know," he sighed. "But it comes with the job..."

"*The lot of a guildsman...*" Dirk mused.

"No," Ing replied. "The lot of *being your friend*."

He pulled Dirk to his feet.

"I'm guessing you're heading for the docks?" he said.

Dirk nodded.

He gestured to the guards that were stationed on the road.

"You think you can help me get through?" he asked.

Ing grimaced.

"I'll try," he said. "Get ready to make a run for it on my signal."

"What signal?" Dirk asked.

"This one..."

Ing vaulted the fence and began running down the street.

The guards saw him and ordered him to stop.

Ing carried on running, and the militiamen chased him down the road.

As soon as they were out of sight, Dirk climbed over the fence and dashed across the street into a snickelway, which led to the Dock.

When he was safely under the cover of darkness, Dirk stopped and said a silent thankyou to the Goddess for helping him.

Ing too, he added, with a warm smile...

* * *

It took him just under an hour to get to the

Docks.

Though the Harbour was less than a mile away, his progress had been slow, and he'd had to dodge several patrols.

He was standing in an alleyway, which lay just off the boardwalk.

The pontoons stood directly ahead.

At the end of one of the jetties, he saw an empty rowing boat.

It appeared unguarded.

If he could get to it, he could use it to escape.

He made his way to the end of the passage and peered around the corner and the Harbourmaster's hut.

It appeared closed and there were no guards in sight.

Fortune was smiling upon him.

He stepped out then skipped along the harbourside toward the pontoon. Then he made his way down the jetty to the boat, and found it tied to a mooring block with a rope.

He stepped down onto the vessel's hull, then began unwinding it from the post.

All of sudden, the door of the Harbourmaster's hut opened, and a man stepped out holding a lantern.

Through the gloom, Dirk noticed that he was wearing a dark green tunic, studded with golden buckles.

It was the uniform of a customs officer.

Dirk froze and crouched low where he was.

He watched in silence as the man began pacing the boardwalk, checking on the ships that were moored to the jetties.

Dirk cursed under his breath.

Maybe his luck was finally running out...?

The man stood up and headed towards the pontoon.

Dirk ducked low and tried not to move.

He heard the officer's footsteps coming towards him.

Suddenly, the man stopped.

"Who's there?" he called. "Horace, is that you?"

Dirk lifted his head.

The lantern was shining directly in his face.

"You're not Horace!" the man retorted.

He went for the dagger at his belt.

Without thinking, Dirk jumped up and seized him by the legs.

The lantern crashed down onto the boardwalk and the knife fell from his hands.

He kicked out and one his boots struck Dirk in the chest.

He reached across the decking for the blade, but Dirk took hold of his foot and pulled him back.

The officer fell into the boat, causing the hull to bob up and down.

Dirk grabbed him by the collar and lifted him up.

In the glow of the moonlight, Dirk saw the man's face.

He was an older man with a grey beard.

He looked scared, terrified.

"Please," he stuttered, "D-don't h-hurt me..."

His reaction was telling. Dirk assumed he'd been briefed about the jailbreak.

"Sit down," he ordered. "Be quiet, and you won't be harmed."

The man did as he said.

Dirk then reached over the boardwalk for the dagger then used it to cut the rope.

"Can you row?" he asked the man.

The customs officer nodded.

"Then get to it."

The man leant down and lifted up the set of oars that had been stored under the thwart. He then threaded the poles through each of the row-locks and began steering the boat out onto the water.

"W-where are we going?" the man asked, as their vessel caught the tide.

"Downriver," Dirk replied.

The man nodded and turned the bow into the current.

Despite his foppish appearance, he handled the boat well, and was proving himself to be a good sailor.

"Not your first time on the water, is it?" Dirk remarked.

"I-I was a crewman with *The Seaguard* for twenty years," he replied.

The Seaguard had been a warship in the Hessellian Navy. Six months ago, it had run aground whilst sailing from the Capital to Ghis... According to the official reports, the Captain had made a grave mistake circumnavigating a bend in the river, but in truth, it had been boarded and then scuttled by Elven Separatists.

"You sail well," Dirk said.

The man nodded and smiled.

"If it was up to me, I'd have never left the navy," he said. "But with the way things are, I've a feeling I'll be safer working on dry land."

The sinking of *The Seaguard* had been the Elves' biggest victory in the war, and the rumours of what had happened had sent ripples of consternation through the towns and cities of the Empire. For the first time since the start of the conflict, the commonfolk were questioning the Emperor's indomitability.

The officer steered the boat into the centre of the river, where it caught the tide and began moving quickly downstream.

He raised the oars out of the water.

"No need for these now," he explained. "Except for steering... This section of the Wynt has always been gentle."

Dirk gave him a nod and sat back against the stern, then turned his eyes to the riverbanks, looking out for guards who had been stationed along the shore.

"May I ask, where it is, we're going?" the man asked. "I've a wife, you see, and she'll be worried if I don't turn in..."

"If I tell you," Dirk replied, "I'll have to kill you."

The man visibly gulped

He spoke no more as they cleared the town walls and progressed down the waterway toward Brynnig, which sat astride the fork of the Wynt and the Wyl. It sat on the county border, so would be a safe place to disembark.

However, doing so would prove risky.

It would mean travelling by foot, which was slow, and without coin, he couldn't hire a horse.

He'd be better off staying in the boat.

But that raised the question of what to do with his unexpected passenger...

He couldn't let him off at Brynnig.

The man would go running to the Guild...

Any later, and the charge of 'kidnapping' would be added to his crime sheet.

Something needed to be done.

"You," Dirk said, "Give me the oars."

The man looked puzzled but did as he was told.

He unhooked them from the rowlock and handed them over.

But Dirk didn't take them.

Instead, he held onto the sides of the boat and began rocking it from left to right.

The man wobbled on his feet.

"What are you doing?" he cried, dropping the oars.

"This is where you get off," Dirk replied.

He rocked the boat harder.

The man lost his balance and fell over the side, landing in the water with a mighty splosh.

His head bobbed to the surface as Dirk sailed away.

He coughed and spluttered but was otherwise unhurt.

"Rascal!" the man yelled, as he frantically began treading water. "I'm going straight to the Guild!"

Go ahead, Dirk thought.

By the time you get there, I'll be in the Capital....

CHAPTER 10

It had been nearly a year since Dirk had last seen the nine spires of St. Lucien's Cathedral. The great structure stood more than a mile away at the centre of the city, its majestic towers of polished stone gleaming in the afternoon sunlight.

He dipped the oars into the water and steered his boat to the riverbank.

He would enter the city by foot.

Landing in the harbour would draw too much attention, and it was imperative his visit went unnoticed.

The craft drifted to the shore and grounded itself in the fine silt. Dirk climbed out, sheathed his stolen dagger and made his way to the road.

It led to the Northern Gate.

It would be easy enough to get through.

Traffic was busy there at the best of times, but even more so during the Harvest.

He joined the road and mingled amongst the

throng of merchants and farmers, who were making their way to the market.

As they approached the gate, the crowd bunched together and slowed to a crawl. Dirk stepped out of the line and saw a troop of soldiers at the gate. They were inspecting the papers of anyone coming in.

"What's going on?" Dirk asked.

A merchant, who was standing alongside him, answered.

"They're checking all travel permits," the man said.

"Why?" Dirk asked.

"Elven spies," the man replied, somewhat conspiratorially. "...Though, to me, I suspect it would be much easier to check everyone's ears..."

He chuckled to himself, laughing at his own joke.

"Do you have a permit?" Dirk asked.

"Of course," the man said, brandishing his papers.

"This is fake," Dirk lied.

The man huffed, shivering his jowls.

"It is not," the man declared. "It was stamped by the Royal Clerk last week!"

Dirk read aloud from the page.

"It says here this permit was issued to Rangill Jurghoof..."

"That's me," the man said.

"So, you claim..." Dirk replied. "But can you prove it?"

The man's cheeks flushed red.

"Who are you to ask, Sir?" he spluttered.

Dirk pointed to the Iron Seal on his chest.

"The Guild," he replied. "And if you don't give me an answer, I'll be forced to arrest you."

The man suddenly became meek.

"No, No," he said. "There's no need for that. I'm sure we can come to some arrangement...."

He reached into his pocket and pulled out a purse.

"What's this?" Dirk asked. "A bribe?"

The man froze.

He appeared petrified.

"That cloak you're wearing," Dirk said. "Where did you get it?"

"Corrine's," the man replied. "In the *Einshoon*."

The Einshoon was a wealthy district in the north of Kronnig, famous for its expensive Boutiques.

"Could she vouch for you?" Dirk asked.

"Oh yes," the man replied. "She knows me well."

Dirk cut his eyes at the man.

"Ok," he says. "Hand me your cloak."

The man removed it from his shoulders and gave it to Dirk.

"...Now wait here," he said, "while I check out your story."

"Y-yes sire," the man replied.

He remained rooted to the spot as Dirk

moved up the line.

As soon as he was out of the man's sight, he threw the cloak over his shoulders and fastened the buttons at the front.

It was long, warm and luxurious.

Providing he could keep his uniform covered, it would offer a good disguise.

He followed the throng to the gate, where he was stopped by one of the guards, who asked him for his permit.

Dirk handed them the Merchant's scroll.

The man unfurled it then eyed him suspiciously, before handing it back and waving him through.

Dirk breathed a sigh of relief then stepped through the gate, where he found himself on the *Nordenstrasse*, a wide thoroughfare which led to the *Imperialplatz*.

He followed the throng to the square, which was full of farmers, who were selling all manner of foods that had harvested from the nearby fields, or foraged from the Emperor's Forest, which lay to the north. At its centre was the Fountain of Errant Star, named in honour of the comet that had heralded the Emperor's birth.

Its base was hexagonal, representing the six counties of Gerwald, and its spout was surrounded by effigies of *Murkwolds*, legendary river-dwelling creatures who had bodies of men and the heads of fish.

A cadre of troubadours surrounded it, playing on their lutes to the delight of the children who were dancing at their feet.

The grand frontage of St. Lucien's stood behind them, its looming towers casting nine long shadows across the plaza. They pointed towards the Guildschool, which stood on the opposite side of the square.

Dirk gave it a glance as he passed it by, fondly remembering the six years he'd spent there, learning his trade.

Standing beside it was the *Emperor's Legs*, a tavern popular with the recruits, which was owned by a former Guildsman named Bartheld.

As he approached, he noticed it was closed.

A sign was hanging from door, which read, *Shut for Cleaning - Come back Tomorrow.*

Dirk smiled.

If the Emperor's Legs was closed for cleaning, it would be a first.

The Inn had a notorious reputation for being squalid and cheap, two things that made it endearing to the begrimed and penniless recruits who were the main source of its custom.

He made his way to the window and looked inside.

The decor looked unchanged since his last visit.

The furniture was still chipped and stained, the carpets worn and dirty, and the walls were broken and cracked.

The only thing missing was Bartheld himself.

He wrapped on the window and waited.

Nothing stirred inside.

Then he noticed a glint of candlelight coming from the back room.

He knocked on the window again, but it was clear that whoever it was inside, didn't want to be disturbed.

The light was fading as the evening drew in.

Dirk shivered on the spot.

In the twilight, he made his way around the side of the building to investigate the source of the light.

Peering through the window, he saw the unmistakable figure of the Innkeep sitting at a table in the back room. He was accompanied by Major Patz, the one-armed Drill Sergeant, who'd taught Dirk how to fight.

He sneered at the sight of him.

The man had betrayed him in Einhof, speaking against him during the trial of Guildsergeant Bakker.

His false testimony had nearly cost Dirk his life.

The two men were drinking from a flagon and appeared to be friends.

Dirk wondered how they knew other.

He waited where he was, watching them through the glass, daring not to reveal himself, for fear of being recognised.

Patz was a brute of a man and there was unfinished business between them.

But now was not the time nor place.

He made his way back to the front of the Inn, then waited in the shadows as the night fell around him.

Several hours later, he saw the glow of candlelight moving through the bar. Moments later, the door opened, and the Major stepped out. After exchanging a few words with Bartheld, he shook the man's hand then began making his way across the square to the Guildschool.

The Innkeep closed the door and returned inside.

Once Patz was out of the sight, Dirk approached the window and wrapped on the glass.

"Bartheld," he called. "Are you in there?"

The grizzled face of the ex-Guildsman peered at him from behind the pane.

Dirk dropped his hood.

"Bartheld," he said. "It's me. Open up."

"Dirk?" the man mouthed.

He nodded.

The Innkeep made his way to the door and lifted the latch.

Dirk came inside, rubbing the chill from his arms.

"Recruit Vanslow," the man said, "What brings you here?"

"It's Guildsman Vanslow, now," Dirk replied, pulling aside his cloak to reveal the Iron Seal sewn into his tunic. "...And I need your help."

Bartheld nodded and beckoned him inside.

* * *

"It's a strange ask..." Bartheld remarked, as he poured a measure of *Einhof Sweet* into a glass and offered it to Dirk. "Are you sure you want to do this?"

Dirk took the rum and gulped it down.

"It's the only way I can prove my innocence," he replied.

"But seeking out Ruul Zamar..." the Innkeep mused, "It's akin to suicide."

"I have no other choice," Dirk said. "Without a confession from his assassin, I'll be tried and hanged for Grand Arson...."

"Not to mention Vow-Breaking," the man added.

Dirk shuddered at the thought.

He'd already stood trial at one Guild Court. He didn't want to suffer a second.

"It seems you understand my predicament..." he groaned.

Bartheld nodded.

"I do," he said. "And I wouldn't wish it on my worst enemy."

Dirk placed the empty glass on the table.

"So, will you help me?" he asked.

"Aye," the man said. "If you can call it *help*..."

He took a seat on the bench opposite Dirk and sipped from his tankard.

"There's a Tavern in the Eastern Quarter

called the *Westren Star*," he began. "I've heard rumours that Ruul and his companions meet there to plot their schemes."

The man smiled resignedly.

"...But there's no way they'll let you in looking like that," he finished, pointing to Dirk's tunic. "Unless...."

Bartheld's word drifted away.

He seemed deep in thought.

"Unless what?" Dirk pressed.

"Unless you tell them your name is 'Mikken'," he replied.

"Mikken?" Dirk said. "Who's that?"

"No one knows," Bartheld replied, with a smile. "...And that's the beauty of it."

He stood up and poured another shot of rum.

Dirk looked at him, confused.

"*Mikken* is a codename," Bartheld explained, "...for an informer within the Guild. He's been passing on our secrets to Ruul's cabal for several years, advising them of our operations, and whatnot..."

He corked the bottle then placed it down.

"...If you go there, claiming to be him," he said, "...Ruul will meet you for sure."

He picked up the glass and handed it to Dirk.

"What if he doesn't believe me?" he asked.

Bartheld's lips parted into a grim smile.

"Then it'll be a short meeting..." he replied.

CHAPTER 11

After saying his farewells to Bartheld, Dirk left The Emperor's Legs and made his way east across the city to the haunt of Ruul Zamar.

The gangster had a fearsome reputation and had evaded the clutches of the Guild for many years. Dirk knew little about him, save for the fact that he was old, and that he ruled over his syndicate with an iron fist.

His gang, who called themselves *The Night Owls*, had been responsible for many notable crimes in Gerwald, including the theft of the crown jewels from the Tower of Kronnig, and the murder of Prince Lansig at his palace in Bryn.

They were well-organised and notoriously secretive group.

Turncoats and traitors were rare.

Those who were caught and questioned said precious little.

Most said nothing at all.

When asked about Ruul, all that had ever been said was that he came from Kulaani, and that his skin was adorned with a quilt of tattoos.

Dirk painted a picture of the man in his mind.

He imagined him to be tall and dark, with piercing brown eyes.

As he passed through *Leissen Row* and into the Eastern District, he wondered how close this would be to the truth...

* * *

The Westren Star stood at the end of the crossroads of *Greta Street* in a dingy part of town. A statue of the eponymous Saint had been erected at the centre of the junction.

Dirk had read about her in the Testament.

She was known as the *Prophet of Doom,* as it was said she had the power of foresight. She'd used it on the Eve of Solstice to warn V'Loire that if he didn't leave Shida, he would die on the morrow at the hands of his friends. St. Rinda had famously scoffed at her words, dismissing them as hokum... But she was proved right the next day, when the Elven Magus, Hexis, seized the Prophet from his home, and then had him stoned to death by his disciples.

Dirk smiled ruefully.

If only he could see the future himself...

Then he'd have an idea of what awaited him.

He approached the Tavern's iron braced door

and rang the bell that was hanging from the awning above it.

Moments later, a sliding hatch opened just above his waist.

Dirk crouched down and peered through the slot.

A pair of bright yellow eyes looked back at him.

"What do you want?" a voice asked on the other side.

"I've come to see Ruul," Dirk replied.

"Ruul?" the voice answered. "No one by that name here, *Guildsman*..."

The figure closed the hatch.

Dirk gritted his teeth and rang the bell again.

The slider opened.

"Go away," the voice said. "There's nothing for you here."

"I need to see Ruul," Dirk repeated. "Tell him it's Mikken."

The yellow eyes widened.

"Mikken?" the voice asked.

"Yes," Dirk replied. "And I'm in a hurry, so don't keep me waiting."

The figure on the other side closed the hatch.

Dirk then heard a key being turned in the lock.

The door creaked open.

Standing behind it was a tiny humanoid, no more than three foot tall.

It looked vaguely like a Dwarf but without

the pronounced features.

"What are you?" Dirk asked.

The Halfling fixed him a glare.

"I'm a Sprite," he replied. "And you should mind your manners!"

"I'm sorry," Dirk said. "I've never seen one of your kind before."

"Not many people have," the Sprite replied. "Our folk live deep in the forests, away from the likes of you."

"I meant no offence," Dirk said.

"Then it's lucky for you that none was taken."

He stepped away from the door and beckoned Dirk inside.

He crossed the threshold and found himself in a small hallway, which sat at the foot of a staircase. To his right was a door with a glass panel. Behind it was a bar, where people were drinking.

"This way," the Sprite said.

He turned around and approached the stairs.

Dirk followed him gingerly.

"Why isn't Ruul at the bar?" he asked.

"He doesn't drink," the Sprite replied, as he huffed and puffed up the steps. "It's one of the reasons he's lived so long..."

He began tittering to himself, but Dirk wasn't sure why.

He hadn't told a joke, and if he had, it wasn't funny.

"Are all Sprites as kooky as you?" Dirk asked, as they reached the top.

The pixie laughed.

"No," he chuckled. "Most are dull and boring."

"So, you're the exception?"

The Sprite smiled.

"Exceedingly so," he beamed.

He danced across the landing to a door which stood at the end of the corridor.

"In here," he said, grinning.

A wave of trepidation crossed Dirk's mind.

Something didn't feel right.

It felt like he was being led into a trap.

He froze on the spot.

"What's wrong?" the Sprite asked. "Are you scared?"

"No," Dirk lied.

"Then come forward," the little man replied. "The one you seek is behind this door."

Dirk took a breath and stepped forward.

He took hold of the door handle and turned it.

"Now go inside," the Sprite said.

Dirk pushed open the door.

The room was dark.

Thick curtains covered the windows, blocking out the light.

"There's no one here," Dirk said.

"There is," the Sprite replied. "Go in and take a look."

Dirk steeled himself and went inside.

He didn't notice the tripwire until he'd set it off...

It triggered a crossbow that had been set against the far wall.

Dirk felt the dart pierce the flesh of his chest.

He winced and pulled it out.

The point was no longer than an inch but was coated in a greenish liquid, which smelled of aniseed.

He turned and faced the Sprite.

"What's this?" he growled. "Some sort of trick?"

The Sprite's lips parted into a wicked smile.

Dirk drew the dagger from his belt.

The Sprite backed away, then turned and hurried down the corridor toward the stairs.

Dirk followed him, but after taking no more than two strides, his legs suddenly felt heavy.

He suddenly realised that the dart had been poisoned.

He dropped to his knees as a peculiar numbness spread across his body and down his arms.

He crumbled to the floor and cursed the Sprite for his ruse.

"I'll get you for this..." he muttered, the words tumbling from his lips.

His head dropped to the floor.

He couldn't move.

He felt the numbness seeping up his neck and into his face.

He started to choke.

He couldn't breathe.

His eyes began to close...

Everything went black.

* * *

Dirk came to and found himself hanging upside down inside what appeared to be the windshaft of a mill.

A stream of bright sunlight shone through the cracks in the shutters, alighting the whirling cogs and creaking wheels, which were turning all around him.

His face felt hot, a symptom of the blood that had pooled inside his head.

How long had he been hanging here?

He looked up at his ankles.

They had been bound with rope, which had been fixed to a beam in the cap.

The Mill's grinder lay beneath him, two granite blocks that whirled together on a shaft. The stones were huge and were spinning in time with the cogs.

A metal slide lay over it.

Large chunks of ore were trickling down it into the grinder, where they were crushed into gravel.

"Looks like he's awake," a voice behind him growled.

Dirk turned his head toward it and saw two men sitting on a beam.

They looked rascally and dangerous, the kind of characters you wouldn't want to meet on a dark night.

"Finally..." the other man sneered. "We've been waiting here for hours."

His voice was shrill and weaselly.

Dirk watched as they got up and made their way toward him along a narrow gangplank.

"What's going on?" Dirk asked. "Where am I?"

"Kruger's Mill," the first man said.

Dirk knew of the place.

It lay several miles to the west of the city, near the *Oswald Downs*.

It was remote and off the beaten path.

The perfect place to have someone killed.

"...But soon you'll be down there," the second man added, chuckling snidely.

Dirk glanced below him at the crusher.

He was directly above it.

The first man reached inside his tunic and produced a knife.

"What are you doing?" Dirk asked, his voice laced with panic.

"Cutting you free," the first man answered.

"Master Ruul likes his victims to be awake while they die," the second man explained. "...So, they don't miss anything."

His companion placed his blade against the rope.

He then started sawing through the line.

"Wait!" Dirk begged. "I'm Mikken! The informer! I work for you."

"Pull the other one," the weaselly man re-

A VOW OF SUCCOUR

plied. "Mikken's one-armed. You clearly have two."

Dirk glanced up.

The rascal's knife had nearly bitten through half the rope.

"Ok," Dirk said. "You're right! I lied."

"So, who are you then?" the second man asked.

Dirk needed to think fast.

"Rangill Jurghoof," he cried.

He reached inside his tunic and produced the trader's travel permit.

"Here," he said. "Proof."

The man took the document and studied what it said, while his companion continued cutting.

After what seemed like an eternity, the man lifted his head.

"If that's who you are," he said, "why are you dressed like a Guildsman?"

"It's my brother's jacket..." Dirk yelled. "He told me about Mikken. He said if I wore it and said I was him, Ruul would see me..."

The man rubbed his chin.

"Why do you want to see him?"

"Business," Dirk replied, as the cords of rope began fraying above him. "I need someone killed! I'm willing to pay...!"

"Well, I guess that's just too bad," the man replied. "Because we have orders to kill you. ...And no one disobeys the boss."

Dirk glanced up at the rope.

It was nearly cut through.

Just then, the Sprite appeared at the edge of the beam.

He called out to the two men.

"Pogar, Jonnis," he said. "You're to go to the Storehouse at once. Ruul has a job for you."

The man holding the knife stopped.

"But we're not finished here," the other man said.

"He wants you there now," the Sprite replied.

The man holding the knife withdrew his blade and placed it inside his pocket. The other man shrugged his shoulders and sighed.

"Come on, Pogar," he whistled. "Orders-is-orders..."

The two men made their way across the beam to a ladder that led to the lower floors.

The Sprite watched them climb down and exit before he turned to Dirk.

"What was that you were saying about business?" he asked.

"Like I told you before," Dirk replied. "I'll only speak to Ruul..."

The Spite sniffed, then smiled.

"Very well," he said. "What do you have to say?"

Dirk gave him a confused look.

He couldn't comprehend what the Sprite was saying.

Then it suddenly dawned on him.

"You're Ruul Zamar?" he asked.

The Sprite nodded.

"I may not look the part," he replied, "But I assure you, I'm every bit as fearsome as my reputation suggests."

Dirk looked at him, bewildered.

"I thought Ruul Zamar was Kulaanian..." he gasped.

"So does everyone else..." the Sprite replied, "...which is why it's been so easy to keep my true identity a secret."

Dirk gave him a nod of appreciation.

It was genius.

No one looking at the Sprite would expect him to be anything but a footstool.

It was the perfect disguise and explained why he'd evaded capture for so long. If his physiology was anything like a Dwarf's, it also explained his longevity.

"So," Ruul began, "You said something about business? A matter of having someone killed?"

Dirk nodded.

"Who?"

"He's from Durnborg," Dirk said.

"Fine," Ruul replied. "His name?"

"He's a powerful man..." Dirk added. "It won't be easy."

Ruul shook his head and smiled.

"It matters not," he said. "As long as he lives and breathes, we can make it otherwise so."

He leaned forward and looked him in the eye.

"Now tell me..." he said. "What is his name?"

Dirk sighed.

"Kurgen Mollat..."

A twisted smile crossed Ruul's cheeks.

"Very well," he said. "The night after tomorrow, it shall be done."

"What about payment?" Dirk asked. "Don't you want Gold?"

The Sprite laughed.

"When you're as rich as I am, you trade in less tangible than coins and trinkets."

Dirk looked at him, confused.

"Then what do you want?" he asked.

"Favours," Ruul replied. "If I do this thing for you, you'll repay my generosity with obedience. From this point forth, you'll be mine. You'll follow my orders, obey my commands. Your life will belong to me. Agreed?"

It was a huge price to ask.

But Dirk had no choice.

"Agreed," he said.

Ruul smiled.

"...On one condition," Dirk added.

The Sprite raised an eyebrow.

"Go on," he said.

"This man, Mollat, betrayed me," Dirk replied. "I want him to suffer a traitor's death."

Ruul smiled wickedly.

"You want him strangled?"

Dirk nodded.

"Then you're in luck," the Sprite said. "I've the perfect man for the job... Or should I say... *woman*."

CHAPTER 12

After being freed from his bonds, Dirk was taken outside where he found one of Ruul's men waiting for him, with a horse.

"A gift from Mr Zamar," he said. "To help you find your way home."

Dirk gave him a nod then climbed up into the saddle.

The man handed him the reigns.

"I'm to tell you that he may come calling on you at any time," he said. "So be prepared."

"I'll keep an eye out," Dirk replied.

He dug his heels into the horse's sides and led it up the track to the quarry's entrance. From there, he followed the path towards Kronnig, before turning west onto the Northern Highway...

* * *

The following evening, just before sunset, he sighted the Durnborg town walls. Quickening his pace, he steered his horse toward Mollat Manor.

As he got closer, he noticed workers in the fields of the estate.

They were busy erecting stalls, installing fences, and hanging bunting for the Erntfest.

To avoid being seen, so he dismounted and approached the manor directly from the south.

A small wood surrounded the house at its rear.

It was dense and overgrown, so he set loose his steed and ventured inside alone.

Clawing his way through the thicket, he eventually came to a small wall, which he presumed marked the boundary of the Manor's garden. Following it round to the left, he came to a section that had fallen down. He clambered over the rubble into the yard beyond, where he found a cobblestone path, which was covered in tendrils. He followed it north towards the manor, and came to a conservatory, which stood at the rear of the house.

Its sides were covered with panes of glass that were cracked and broken by the branch of a tree, which had been allowed to grow through it.

Dirk carefully ducked through the frame and approached the outside door.

He turned the handle.

It didn't move.

He noticed that the latch was stiff and covered in rust.

It couldn't be jimmied open, so he gave it a

sharp kick with the heel of his boot.

The panel shattered on its hinges.

Dirk moved it aside then stepped through the gap, where he found himself in a living room at the rear of the house.

It was dark inside, and the air smelled of death.

Dirk covered his nose as he moved through the room, passing by the antique chairs and chestnut cabinets, which were covered in a decade's worth of dust.

Against the far wall was a door.

He opened it and stepped out into a corridor, which led to the lobby.

Following it round, he found himself at the bottom of the staircase.

Glancing up, he saw the balustrade that fenced the landing, noticing the notch in the wood that had been made by Mollat's noose.

He shuddered at the memory of the man's corpse hanging there, with his blue skin and bulging eyes.

Casting the thought from his mind, he quietly made his way up the stairs, thinking through his plan.

Not that he had much go to on...

All he knew was that the assassin was coming tonight...

And that he had to take her alive.

Obtaining her confession was paramount.

It would vindicate him and see him return to

his life at the Guild.

But if he failed, it meant a life on the run.

What made things harder was that she'd come expecting a trap.

That was for certain.

She'd already killed Mollat once, at the behest of Klept.

No doubt she'd be wary if asked to do it a second time...

Her caution would make her dangerous, so his plan would need to be fool proof.

As he passed the boxes on the landing, he noticed Mummer's Dummy amongst the junk.

It was the size of a man, with two arms and two legs.

He wondered if he could use it to trick her.

He picked it up and took it into the bedroom.

Mollat's four-poster bed stood before him.

Dirk suddenly had an idea.

He lifted the mannequin onto the mattress, then pulled the sheets over it.

He stepped back.

At a glance it appeared as if a man was sleeping beneath the covers.

But would it would fool her?

Possibly.

All he needed now was a place to hide.

He crouched down and looked under the bed.

It was a good spot, but not the most practical. It would be hard to spring out if he were lying on the floor...

He turned to the cupboard, which was standing against the wall.

It was big enough for him to fit inside, but in order to remain out of sight, he'd have to close the door, but opening it would make a sound, which would alert her to his presence...

He turned to the curtains.

They were thick and long.

He could hide behind them in a standing position. They wouldn't make a noise when he jumped out.

He stepped into the window's bay and closed the curtains behind him, leaving a gap in the fabric through which he could see.

It afforded him a clear view of the run of the floor, from the door to the bed.

It seemed the perfect spot.

He stood and waited for the assassin to appear.

He didn't know what time she'd show but he needed to be ready for her when she did.

He only had one chance to get this right.

If he failed, all hope for him was lost.

He shifted on his feet to make himself comfortable.

He could be in for a long night...

As he stood there, frozen to the spot, he began second guessing himself, wondering whether he'd chosen the right place?

For all intents and purposes, behind the curtains was the ideal place to hide.

But was it too obvious?

* * *

Several hours later, Dirk heard the creaking of a window being opened downstairs.

From his hiding spot, he listened intently as the assassin climbed through the fenestra and made her way across the lobby to the stairs.

"I know you're in here," she called out, to no one in particular.

Her accent was tinted with an aureate tone.

She sounded harmless.

But Dirk knew she wasn't.

He remembered reading her charge sheet in the records room.

The woman was a cold-blooded killer through-and-through.

"If you come out now, I promise I won't hurt you," she said

It was a lie.

Dirk heard her ascending the stairs.

"...All I want to do is talk." she said.

Her footsteps crossed the landing.

She came into the bedroom.

She was taller and broader than most women, and had a long mane of fiery red hair, which was tied behind her head in a bun.

"...I just want to know why you've brought me here," she added, drawing a garrot wire from the fabric of her sleeve.

She looked at the bed, studying it for a moment.

Then she glanced at the curtain and smiled.

"...I want to know why I've been asked to kill someone..." she continued, stretching out the wire in her hands, "... who's already dead."

In a flash, she darted forward and aimed a high kick through the gap in the curtain.

The figure standing behind it stumbled then fell forward.

With incredible speed, she twisted the wire into a loop, then thrust it over his head.

Then she twisted her body behind him and drew the cords tight.

At once it was clear she realised something wasn't right.

The man she was garrotting was making no attempt to fight back.

A look of puzzlement beguiled her face.

She let go of her victim.

The Mummer's Dummy fell to the floor.

Before she could react, Dirk thew aside the bed sheets and sprang up at her from the mattress. He seized her from behind and placed the blade of his dagger against her throat.

"Ertha Rouge," he whispered. "You're under arrest."

* * *

"I don't know what you're trying to do," the

woman sneered, as Dirk shunted her down the stairs. "But if you think any of this will stick in court, you're sadly mistaken..."

Dirk held her by the bonds that tied her wrists.

"...I did nothing wrong."

"You killed Kurgen Mollat," Dirk replied.

"Try proving it," she laughed.

"It'll be easy," he rasped, pushing her towards the door. "...With your confession."

The La Broqian laughed, shivering the waves of curly ginger hair that fell from her crown."

"And why would I confess?" she chuckled.

Dirk opened the door and ushered her outside.

"Because it's the right thing to do," Dirk replied. "...And you'll be given full immunity."

She baulked.

Dirk turned her around and looked her in the eyes.

"I know Klept put you up to this," he said. "Help me bring him in and I'll see you walk free."

She shook her head.

"If I turn work with the Guild, I'm as good as dead," she said.

She had a good point.

By working with the authorities, she would be seen as a traitor to the syndicate, and her life would be forfeit.

"You might as well just let me go," she offered.

Dirk considered her words.

If he released her, it was over.

The same was true if he brought her in but she failed to speak.

It seemed all hope was lost.

He was damned either way.

Suddenly, he had an idea.

"What if we could compromise?" he said.

Rouge smiled.

"How it that possible when I hold all the cards?"

"Not all," Dirk replied.

She gave him a cursory look.

"You were sent here to kill Mollat," he began. "But he was already dead, because you'd already killed him."

"How does that change anything?" she scoffed.

"Ruul runs a tight ship," Dirk replied. "Nothing happens without his say so."

He stared into her eyes.

"What do you think he'd do," he continued, "if he were to know you killed Mollat without his permission?"

"He'd kill you," she spat. "For lying to him."

"Then he'd kill you," Dirk replied.

She curled her lip in disgust.

He'd made his point and made it well.

"You'd see us both dead?" she asked.

Dirk nodded.

She studied his face.

Her lips parted into a cruel smile.

"Orc Shit," she sneered. "You're bluffing."

Dirk snorted.

"Am I?" he said. "I'm a wanted a man. If I can't prove Klept's guilt, I'll be swinging from a gibbet by the end of the month."

The blood drained from her cheeks.

She could see he wasn't lying.

"Ok," she groaned. "...this compromise of yours? What do you have in mind?"

CHAPTER 13

Dirk followed Ertha through the rushes that braced the riverbank.

They kept themselves low to the ground, under the cover of the shadows cast by the town's walls, whose battlements glowed from the light of lanterns, carried by guards.

They were heading for a secret entrance into Durnborg via the sewers. Ertha had told him about it before they'd left the Manor, and though he hated the thought of wading through filth it seemed a much safer option than taking their chances at the gates.

"How much further?" he whispered to the assassin, who was a few yards in front.

"Not far now," Ertha replied, glancing back at him over her shoulder. "The passage is just up ahead."

She lay down amongst the reeds and shimmied forward on her belly.

Dirk aped her movements and crept up beside her.

She pointed to a small hole that had been cut at the base of the walls.

A narrow canal had dug into the earth beneath it.

It led to the river and was full of water.

"There it is," she said.

The hole was covered with a grate and looked barely wide enough to squeeze through.

"That's it?" Dirk asked, his voice laced with incredulity

Ertha nodded.

"But it's too small," he replied. "And it's blocked with bars."

"It's just for show," she replied. "The grate is hinged and it's wider on the inside."

Dirk gave her a puzzled look.

"Why's that?" he asked

"Because it's not really a sewer," she replied, with a smile. "It's an escape tunnel."

Dirk shook his head in disbelief.

"During the Civil War," she explained, "the Duke of Durnborgschaft had it built to escape the Imperialists."

Dirk had heard of the conflict.

Formally known as the *War of Ascension*, it had been fought between the Northern Duchies and the Unionists in the early 1100's, and its resolution saw the creation of the Gerwaldian Empire in its current form.

By all accounts, the conflict had been a savage

one.

Thousands had died, including many of the Dukes and their families.

"Did he ever use it?" Dirk asked.

She smiled grimly.

"He never had chance," she replied. "He was betrayed by one of his footmen before the Emperor's forces stormed the gates."

"So how do you know of it?" he asked.

She gave him a knowing look.

"The Night Owls know a lot of things," she said with a wink.

They waited for the guards on the walls to pass, then slid down the embankment into the muddy water of the canal. Wading through the gunk, they made their way up to the hole in the wall.

"Give me a boost," she said.

He cupped his hands together and held them between his legs.

Ertha raised her leg out of the water and placed the heel of her boot across his palms.

With a heave, he lifted her up and she took hold of the grate.

She then gave it a shunt and it creaked on its hinges and swung inwards.

She looked down at him and smiled.

"We're in," she said.

She reached down and he took her hand.

She then hauled him up to the breach.

Dirk looked into the tunnel.

A wall of blackness stared back.

"How will we see?" he asked.

Ertha slid her hand inside a pouch at her belt and produced a cylindrical tube, which looked like a candle.

She stepped inside the tunnel then struck the end of it against the wall.

It produced a spark, and the tube began fizzing.

Seconds later the tip was sparkling with a phosphorate flame.

Its glow was strong enough to light up the passage.

"I got this from a Sewerman in Tibrut," she said. "They have problems there with *Mukhtars*."

Mukhtars were strange creatures that lived in the catacombs beneath many towns and cities. Though Dirk had never seen one himself, he'd heard that they were short, stunty humanoids with the faces of rats.

"I hope we don't come across any in here," he said.

"We won't," the assassin replied, with a grin. "They only live in the Southern lands. It's cold for them up here."

Dirk followed her along the tunnel, crouching down to avoid hitting his head on the low roof, as the passage veered to the right.

The further they progressed, the wetter the walls became, and water was dripping down from the ceiling.

One of the droplets splashed down on Dirk's forehead.

As he wiped it away, he caught a whiff of it.

It was putrid.

Dirk surmised that the passage had been dug beneath the main sewer.

"Don't let any of the water get into your mouth," Ertha warned. "Or you'll catch the River Sickness and be ill for a month."

"I'll try not to," Dirk replied, mopping the dirty liquid from his forehead.

"How far does this tunnel go?" he asked, staring ahead into the abyss.

"All the way to ruins of the old citadel," she replied.

The broken fortress lay on the eastern side of town, just inside the walls. Ing had told him that it had once been a proud Keep, with a central tower which stood one hundred feet tall. Now, however, only the husk of its walls remained.

They continued down the passage for another several hundred yards, before it abruptly turned to the left.

After turning the corner, they found the way ahead blocked by what appeared to be a rock fall.

"Damn it," Ertha cursed. "There's no way through."

Dirk squeezed past her and examined the wall of stones that stood in their way.

"It looks like a cave-in," Dirk muttered, pointing to the crumbling ceiling above them. "We'll have to go back."

"Wait," she said. "Do you hear that?"

Dirk turned her ear to the sound.

"It sounds like running water," he said.

"Where's it coming from?" she asked.

Dirk closed his eyes and focused on the sound.

"There," he said.

He pointed to the left-hand side of the wall.

Ertha lit the area with her candle.

Dirk crouched down and tapped the bricks with the hilt of his dagger.

"It's hollow," he said.

"You think we can break through?"

With the point of his blade, he began chipping away at the grout that surrounded one of the bricks. When he'd dug enough of it out, he slid his fingertips between the gap and shifted the block from side to side.

Finally, it came loose, and he scooped it free and aside.

Then he placed his face to the hole.

Through the darkness, he saw a trickle of water.

"It's a storm drain," he said excitedly. "We can follow it to the surface..."

He stood up and kicked away the adjacent bricks.

Once he'd made a big enough hole, they climbed through and followed the water up the tunnel, where they soon came to a metallic grate.

Dirk ducked down and looked through the bars.

In the near distance, he saw a line of trees.

They were in *Durn's Park*.

He figured that the water was coming from the stream that flowed through it.

He lifted his boot and kicked at the grate.

It pinged off its rivets and dropped down into the water.

He lay down and crawled through the gap, splashing down into the water on the other side.

He glanced back and saw Ertha sliding out of the passage behind him, the flame of her torch fizzling out touched the water's surface.

Dirk waded to the other side then helped her up onto the bank.

"At least we know where we are now," he said, pushing his hair from his eyes.

"Yes," she agreed. "But, it's a shame we couldn't have found a drier route..."

* * *

They made their way through the park and into the streets of *The Wash*. Keeping to the shadows, they picked their way through the alleys to Greta Street.

"Is that the place?" Ertha asked, gesturing to the casino, which stood on the corner.

Dirk nodded.

"Remember the plan," he said. "I need him

alive."

She scoffed.

"Are you worried I'll accidentally murder him?"

"You are a hired killer..." Dirk replied.

She curled her lip.

"I'm also a professional," she said. "And I take a lot of pride in my work."

Dirk smirked.

"You made mistakes with Mollat," he replied.

She blew out her cheeks.

"What mistakes?"

"You left shards of wood by the bed," Dirk replied. "It was evidence of a struggle."

"Shards," she sniffed. "That proves nothing. The whole house was falling apart..."

"True," Dirk admitted, "But then there was the matter of the noose..."

"There was nothing wrong with the noose," she hissed. "...I tied that knot myself."

"That's where you went wrong..." Dirk replied. "Mollat could only use one of his hands. There's no way he could have done it."

The conviction disappeared from her eyes.

"That fact alone..." he continued. "...proved there was someone else there. So, it just became a matter of connecting the dots."

She huffed and gritted her teeth.

She seemed furious with herself for making such an error.

"Maybe next time," Dirk suggested, "You'll not

leave any loose ends."

She glared at him angrily.

"Oh, don't you worry," she said. "You can be sure of it."

He turned his head to the casino and saw its doors opening. A procession of disorderly scoundrels, rascals and ne'er-do-wells, were being ushered out onto the street by Fryk's Ogre, whose left arm was wrapped in a sling.

"Is that the muscle?" Rouge asked.

Dirk nodded.

"Try not to hurt him if you can," he said. "He may look like a brute, but underneath he's as soft as custard."

She smirked.

"I promise I'll be gentle with him."

When the last of the stragglers left the building, the Ogre returned inside and locked the door.

"Well," she said. "This is where we part. I hope your plans succeeds."

Dirk smiled.

"I hope so too," he replied. "For both our sakes."

She curled her lip and made her way across the street.

Dirk watched from the shadows as she made her way round the building's side, then disappeared through one of the windows.

Everything hinged on her now.

His fate was out of his hands.

He unconsciously reached for the copy of the

She-En which was tucked inside his tunic.

Though its pages were battered and soggy, its touch alone gave him strength.

"Sheenah, help me," he whispered under his breath.

The Goddess answered.

At once, the doors of the building flung open and a shadowy figure darted out into the street.

It was Ertha.

She stopped by the statue of St. Greta and flashed him a winning smile, before disappearing into the shadows, out of sight.

This was his signal.

Dirk quickly ran over to the casino, where he burst through the open doors and made his way down into the pit of the arena.

Hanging from a noose from a window of the office, was the stunted body of Fryk.

The Dwarf was alive, but his face was blue.

He was pulling at the cord that had wrapped around his neck, his legs frantically kicking beneath him in a hangman's jig.

Lying unconscious at his feet was his bodyguard, Klug. The Ogre was on his back, spread-eagled, and snoring like a baby.

Dirk quickly ran to the Dwarf's aid, lifting his legs so that could escape the knot.

He heard Fryk struggling above him, pulling at the cord around his neck. With a determined grunt, slid the line over his chin and promptly crashed to the floor.

The Dwarf gasped, taking in a huge lungful of air.

"V'Loire!" he cried, between breaths. "He wants to kill me... The bastard wants me dead..."

Dirk stood over him.

"Who wants you dead?" he asked.

"Klept..." Fryk whimpered. "I never thought he had it in him.... But now... After this...?"

"I did warn you," Dirk said.

Fryk looked up at him.

"Why are you here?"

"I got word that he'd hired an assassin to kill you," Dirk lied. "Lucky I got here just in time."

The Dwarf got to his feet.

He looked at Klug on the floor then waddled over and gave him a kick.

"Useless ape!" he growled. "Next time I'll hire a Troll!"

Dirk smirked.

"It won't make any difference," he said.

Fryk sniffed.

"There's not a Troll in the world who would allow themselves to be bested by a girl!" he sneered.

"That 'girl'..." Dirk replied. "...Works for Ruul Zamar."

Fryk's face went white.

"Ruul Zamar..." he muttered.

"You've not heard?" Dirk said. "That's who Klept hired to kill you."

The Dwarf shook his head in disbelief.

"V'Loire!" he cried. "I'm a dead man walking..."

"Not necessarily," Dirk replied. "You can always go to the Guild."

Fryk gave him an exasperated look.

"...You want me to testify against Ruul Zamar?" he scoffed.

"No," Dirk replied. "I want you to testify against Klept."

The Dwarf's eyes dropped to the floor.

"It'll ruin me," he sighed. "I'll have to move town and start over."

"You will," Dirk replied. "But it's either that or having to look over your shoulder for the rest of your life..."

"The Dwarf groaned, ruefully.

"Very well," he said. "I've never been one for running. Let's get this over with..."

CHAPTER 14

The bells of Old Joe rang out through the streets as Dirk accompanied Ruystin to the Guildhouse.

Dawn was breaking and the sleepy town had yet to wake, but that didn't stop the Dwarf from fretting about being seen.

He appeared fidgety and kept looking around, fearful that at any point, someone would jump out of the shadows and attack him.

"We need to go faster," he complained. "I'm a sitting duck out here..."

Dirk knew his fears were unfounded, but it was important to keep up the pretence.

At least until he had submitted his statement...

"Don't worry," he said. "We're nearly there..."

"Easy for you to say," Ruystin replied. "You're not the one with the target on your back..."

They turned onto *Provisional Row* and Dirk caught sight of the Guildhouse standing on the corner.

The sight of it made him nervous.

Up until now, everything had gone swimmingly but it was impossible to predict how his comrades would react.

The last time they'd seen him, he was being led away in cuffs by the Town Guards.

He couldn't forget the looks on their faces.

He couldn't forget the look Hamm had given him that night.

The Guildcaptain's face had been a picture of disappointment.

And no wonder...

Guilty or not, Dirk had brought shame to their Order.

His actions had dishonoured them.

But now it was time to put things right...

Dirk took a breath to steel himself as he came to the door.

"Are you ready?" he asked.

The Dwarf sniffed.

"Are you?"

He must have sensed his apprehension.

But it was too late to back out now.

This was it.

The moment of truth.

He swung open the door and boldly marched in.

Errol was manning the reception counter.

The sound of Dirk's footsteps woke him from his nap, and as soon as he saw him, he jumped out of his seat and began ringing the bell that was fixed onto the wall behind him.

It was used for emergencies.

When it was sounded, all Guildsmen in the building were required to assemble at the front desk immediately.

Dirk drew the dagger from his belt and approached the desk.

Errol cowered behind it.

"Don't hurt me," he pleaded. "I didn't mean to abandon you in the records room, I swear."

Dirk grunted and placed the knife on the counter.

"This isn't about the records room," he said, as the room shook to the sound of boots thundering down the stairs.

He glanced at Fryk, who looked confused.

"What's going on?" he said, backing away to the door.

A cadre of Guildsmen appeared at the foot of the stairs.

The Dwarf stopped in his tracks and raised his hands.

Dirk did the same.

The troopers surrounded them both and drew their swords.

Hamm then appeared in the corridor leading to his bunk.

He was half-dressed and half asleep.

But as soon as he laid his eyes on Dirk, his eyes lit up.

"Arrest him," he roared.

The Guildsmen closed in and seized him by the arms.

This wasn't going as well as he'd hoped.

"You've a lot of nerve showing your face here," Hamm snarled.

"I came here willingly," Dirk replied. "To clear my name."

The Guildcaptain laughed.

"Good luck with that," he scoffed. "Your charge sheet's longer than the Rhund!"

"The Dwarf can prove my innocence," Dirk replied.

He pointed at Fryk.

The Dwarf suddenly panicked and ran for the door, but Ing stepped in front of him, barring his way.

He seized the Dwarf by the collar and turned him round.

"...He can also prove Klept's involvement in Mollat's murder," Dirk added.

Everyone's eyes turned to Hamm.

The Guildcaptain grimaced and shifted on his feet.

He was conflicted, unsure of what to do.

"Very well," he said finally. "We'll hear he has to say..."

He turned to the men holding Dirk.

"Take this man to his quarters and confine him there until our interrogation is complete."

Dirk breathed a sigh of relief as the men led him away.

As he was ushered up the stairs, he glanced at Ing and gave him a nod.

His friend returned the gesture with a roll of his eyes.

* * *

Dirk sat on his bunk resting his elbows on his knees.

A million thoughts ran through his head.

The one that concerned him most was the Dwarf's resolve. If Fryk refused to testify, all his efforts would have been for nought...

It concerned him that the interrogation was taking so long.

He'd been locked in his room for several hours now, and he had no idea how things were progressing.

He started to despair.

Another half hour passed.

Things weren't looking good.

Just then, he heard the sound of footsteps outside, followed by the turning of the key in the lock.

The door opened to reveal the sullen jowls of the Guildcaptain.

Dirk got to his feet and gave him a weary salute.

Hamm came in.

In his hands was a warrant scroll.

As soon as Dirk saw it, he feared the worst.

The Dwarf had sold him out.

He wondered what Fryk had told them, and whether kidnapping and extortion had now been added to his list of crimes.

"After interrogating the witness," Hamm said, "I made a visit to the Magistrate."

Dirk's heart sunk in his chest.

It was all over.

He'd soon be taken back to the cells, where he would await his execution.

"After discussing the details of your case," the Guildcaptain continued, "He's agreed to commute all charges."

Hamm handed him the scroll.

Dirk unfurled it.

It was a full pardon, signed by the Magistrate and stamped with the Emperor's seal.

"He's also issued a warrant for the arrest of Burgomeister Klept."

Dirk looked up from the page.

"It seems you were right about him," Hamm said. "The man was rotten to the core... Fryk's provided us with all the evidence we need to bring him in for questioning."

He went on to explain how Klept had been gaming the town coffers since he first took office, using public money to fund a gambling habit that had left him with a mountain of debt.

The revelation shocked Dirk.

During his encounter with the Burgomeister at the Town Hall, the man had painted a picture of himself as being a misguided philanthropist, who had only resorted to murder through happenstance.

But his tale had been a brazen lie.

He was nothing more than a common thief and a liar.

"Where is he now?" Dirk asked.

"The *Erntfest*," Hamm replied. "I'm assembling the men to arrest him while he makes his opening speech."

Dirk gave him a cursory look.

"But Sir," he said, " I got the impression you wanted to bow out quietly?"

"Not anymore," he replied. "For too long I've turned a blind eye to the happenings of this place."

He sighed and averted his eyes.

"I was of the belief that this was a quiet town, where nothing ever happened. But I was wrong... So, in my last action as Guildcaptain, I want to make amends."

"Your *last action*?" Dirk said.

Hamm nodded.

"I've decided to resign my commission," he said. "I've recommended Vargas as my replacement. He's capable and experienced. The men respect him. But of course, if he accepts, we'll need a new Guildsergeant."

He looked Dirk in the eye.

"If the job is offered," Hamm asked. "Would you take it?"

"I'd be honoured, Sir," Dirk replied.

"Good," the Guildcaptain replied. "Now ready yourself for action. We have work to do."

CHAPTER 15

The midday sun shone brightly in the sky as all thirty men of the Durnborg Guild made their way through the Southern Gate and onto the fields of Mollat's estate.

Guildcaptain Hamm was leading from the front, marching so quickly that the men behind him were struggling to keep up.

Dirk brought up the rear, alongside Ing, who seemed a little concerned by their commander's new-found vigour.

"What's got into him?" he remarked, gesturing to the Captain. "He looks like a man possessed."

"He is," Dirk replied, warmly.

The column turned off the road and onto the field, which bustled with people.

Nearly every citizen of Durnborg was here, their numbers bolstered further by those who had come from the outlying villages and farmsteads. There were famous faces too, such as a Armil Grynn, who headed the Agricultural Union, and

Ralph Olberwalt, the champion prize fighter, from Berghof.

The people were bustling around market stalls, manned by farmers, who were selling their produce to traders, merchants and citizens. Dotted in between were corrals containing horses, pigs, and cows. They were fronted with small boxes, where auctioneers stood taking bids on the livestock from people in the crowd.

The stalls and pens were arranged in the shape of a large horseshoe around a central carnival, whose attractions were clustered around a Big Top, dashed with bright red stripes. Many young adults and children were milling around it, enjoying the rides, playing games and laughing and dancing with soldiers of the town guard.

At the far end of the field was a stage.

The Burgomeister was standing upon it addressing a large crowd, and once again looked to be in his element.

"Citizens," he declared, somewhat theatrically, "I welcome you all to this year's Erntfest. I'm sure you'll agree with me when I say it's exceeded all our expectations."

The crowd cheered wildly in response, but their adulation quickly subsided when they noticed the grey tunics of Hamm's troops approaching from the rear.

Klept stopped talking and looked at them.

It was clear he was perturbed by the intrusion but was trying not to show it.

Hamm made his way to the front and climbed the steps of the stage.

A wave of murmurs rippled through the crowd.

No one was sure what was happening.

Klept cracked a smile and extended his arm.

"And now," he said, "A few words from our esteemed Guildcaptain, whose timely investigation allowed this event to be staged."

A few people in the crowd started clapping, believing Hamm's appearance was part of the show.

Klept stepped away from the lectern and invited him to speak.

Without so much as a nod, Hamm took to the podium.

"Citizens of Durnborg," he began. "Thank you all for coming here today to celebrate this year's Festival of Harvest."

Dirk was dumbstruck.

What was he saying?

"It's been my honour to serve you these past twenty years," he continued. "...however, it brings me no joy to bring you news of a terrible crime that has been committed in our otherwise peaceful town."

The audience stirred.

Dirk saw many of them looking at each other, wondering what he meant.

"A crime committed against all of you, by someone entrusted to your care."

He reached inside his tunic and produced a scroll, which he unfurled and held up to the crowd.

Hamm then turned and pointed to the Burgomeister.

"Kohn Klept," he loudly declared. "This is a warrant for your arrest, pertaining to the charges of theft, arson... and murder."

The crowd began to boo and hiss.

The Burgomeister stood rooted to the spot, shaking with fear.

Hamm stepped forward and removed the cuffs at his belt.

Klept glanced at the crowd.

The Burgomeister suddenly panicked.

He reached inside his tunic and pulled out a knife.

The crowd gasped.

Hamm froze on the spot.

The Guildsmen at the foot of the stage drew their swords and began making their way up the steps, but they stopped in their tracks when Klept seized Hamm and placed the knife against his throat.

"Back!" the Burgomeister ordered. "Stay where you are!"

Hamm lifted his hands and his troops slowly retreated.

"I want a horse!" the man yelled. "Bring me one, now!"

A horse whinnied at the back of the crowd and he turned to see one of the mares from the corral being led toward to the stage.

"He'll head for bridge," Dirk commented. "Once he's on the other side, there's nothing we can do..."

Ing smirked.

"There's no chance of that," he said. "He'll never get through the crowd."

Suddenly, the air was filled with a loud roar from the East.

Dirk turned his head towards the commons and saw a band of peasants marching toward them. They were armed with rusty swords and pitchforks, and wear wearing bright red bandanas around their heads.

"Down with the Emperor!" the man at the front cried. "Join the Revolution!"

Dirk recognised his face.

It was Nye Yossell, which meant the man behind him were the *Scarlet Faction*.

And this was their uprising.

He watched as the peasant army stormed into the field, where they rushed towards the outlying stalls.

The people gathered around them ran away screaming as the rebels crashed into the vacant stands and kicked them apart, sending grains and potatoes spilling out over the grass.

One of the auctioneers at the pens stood his ground and berated them, but they lifted him from his box and threw him into one of the corrals, where he was attacked by an angry-looking boar.

Some of the town guard rushed over to face them but a mob of peasants armed with scythes came forward to meet them, whirling their blades over the ground at their feet.

A cry rang out, and Dirk saw one of the guardsmen fall, clutching the stub of his leg, which had been severed above the ankle.

The rebels cheered in celebration.

Things were quickly turning ugly.

Dirk glanced toward the stage.

The audience were screaming in panic.

Most of them had turned their heads to see what was going on, and Klept had used the distraction to make his escape.

He pushed the Guildcaptain to the floor then jumped into the saddle of the mare.

"Dirk!" Ing suddenly yelled. "Look out!"

He turned and saw a bottle of rum hurtling towards his head. A flaming rag had been stuffed inside its neck.

He ducked just in time to avoid it.

It shattered on the ground behind him, spilling the liquor over the grass, which was lit by the flames.

The audience started screaming and running in all directions.

Somewhere within the cacophony of sound, he heard Klept yelling at his horse. He turned his head and saw the mare bolt forward, smashing through the wall of Guildsman who had gathered around it.

Dirk watched as the Burgomeister wheeled his steed around the front of the stage then spurred it towards the road, heading for the Southern Gate.

"We have to stop him!" Dirk yelled.

He looked over to the corrals.

One of them contained a team of horses.

But to get to them, he'd have to fight his way through the rebels, who were engaged in a vicious melee with the town guard.

"We need to break through their line," he said, drawing his *Hunter's Bite.*

Ing groaned.

"How did I know you were going to say that..."

Dirk ran forward with Ing on his tail.

Leading with the point of his blade, he darted amongst the fighting men toward the field's edge.

As he entered the fray, he was confronted by a rebel armed with a pitchfork.

"Where do you think you're going, traitor?" the man said.

Dirk recognised the man's voice.

He was one of Nye's comrades, who'd helped him escape from the courthouse.

"Out of my way," Dirk said. "I've no skin in this game."

"Oh, but you do," the man replied. "You betrayed the Revolution. The penalty for that is death!"

He thrust the pitchfork towards Dirk's chest,

but before the prongs could pierce his skin, Ing leapt at him from the side, tackling him to the ground.

The Rhunligger smothered the man with his weight and began beating him with his elbows.

"Thanks," Dirk said.

"Thank me later," Ing yelled. "Go after Klept!"

Dirk gave him a nod as he turned and dashed over to the corral, where he vaulted the fence and leapt onto the back of one of the horses.

It was a black stallion, and it snorted wildly as Dirk grappled with its bit.   The horse blew a jet of air out of its nose and stamped its feet.

"Easy, boy..." he said, patting its neck.

The horse calmed and Dirk settled in the seat.

He dug his heels in its sides and urged it forward.

It bucked and snorted.

Dirk tapped its rump with the flat of his sword and the stallion cantered forward, clearing the fence in a single bound.

He pulled on the horse's reins and wheeled it around to face the melee.

"Yarr!" he roared.

The stallion whinnied then charged forward into the crowd, running down several of the peasant soldiers, who were foolish enough to stand in its way.

At the edge of the field, Dirk turned the horse toward the gate and spurred it into a gallop.

By now, Klept would be half-way through the

town.

It would take a miracle to catch him...

* * *

Clouds gathered in the skies above as Dirk thundered through the town towards the Hellenburg Bridge.

Digging his heels hard into the sides of his steed, he raced through *Provincial Row*, before coming to the main square.

Yelling at the horse to go faster, he flew through the marketplace onto *Boulder's Avenue,* which would lead him to the County crossing.

It worried him that he'd not yet caught sight of Klept.

But as turned his horse into the Avenue, he saw him up ahead.

The Burgomeister's mare must have lost a shoe during his escape, as it appeared to be limping along at a slow canter.

With a final push he'd catch him...

Dirk flicked the reins of his stallion.

The beast snorted beneath him.

It was sweating profusely, teetering on the point of exhaustion.

"Come on boy!" Dirk whispered. "You can do it...."

The horse seemed to understand him.

With a fierce grunt, it found an extra burst of pace.

Dirk fixed his eyes on Klept as the gap between them began to close, shrinking to no more than thirty yards as the Burgomeister's mare stepped upon the bridge.

"Stop where you are!" he roared.

The Burgomeister turned his head and snarled.

Then he yelled at his mare to go faster.

The stricken horse upped its pace, hobbling along the bridge as fast as it could.

Dirk slowed his stallion as it came into the turn then wheeled it around onto the crossing's wooden slats.

The horse's hooves rocked the bridge as it thundered forward.

Klept was now only yards away.

But so was the end of the bridge...

Dirk's heart sank.

He wouldn't make it.

The Burgomeister was bound to escape.

But just then, Klept made a fatal mistake.

Believing Dirk was right behind him, he struck the rump of his mare with what he believed to be the flat of his dagger. However, the knife had turned in his hand, so instead of whipping his blade against the horse's skin, he stabbed it in the rump with its point.

The mare shrieked and bucked.

Klept was thrown around in his seat.

Dirk seized his chance.

He drew himself alongside the Burgomeister's horse and leapt out of his saddle.

As he flew through the air, he extended his arms and wrapped them round Klept's neck.

The Burgomeister was pulled from his horse.

Both men fell together, hitting the rail of the bridge, before dropping over the side.

Dirk hit the water first and sunk beneath the waves.

The Burgomeister followed him in.

Dirk swam to the surface and caught his breath.

Klept surfaced a few yards from him.

The man was coughing and choking.

Dirk wasn't sure if he could swim.

He swam over and grabbed the man by the shoulder.

"Relax," he said. "I won't let you drown."

The Burgomeister roared and kicked.

His head dipped beneath the surface.

Dirk ducked under and swam towards him.

He took Klept by the underarms and started kicking his legs.

The Burgomeister struggled then stopped when he realised Dirk wasn't going to harm him.

He dragged the man to the surface, where he gasped at the air.

"Don't move," Dirk growled. "Or you'll pull us both under."

The man relaxed his body, and Dirk swam them both to the side.

"Thank you," Klept said, as he hauled himself

up onto the bank.

"Don't thank me," he spat. "I'm placing you under arrest."

Klept palmed away the hair from his face and smiled.

"I' don't think so," he said.

He gestured toward the bridge.

Dirk glanced back and saw they were on the wrong side of the bank.

His heart sunk in his chest.

"I'm so sorry," the Burgomeister said, his words laced with sarcasm. "But I'm afraid you'll be going back to your friends empty-handed."

Dirk shook his head.

He wanted nothing more than to draw his dagger and plunge it into the man's chest.

But that wouldn't be justice.

"There's no use running," Dirk growled. "We'll be sending warrants to every Guild in Gerwald."

Klept laughed.

"Good luck with that," he sneered. " By the time you've got all the requisite paperwork stamped and signed, I'll be long gone."

Dirk cursed under his breath.

He knew he was right.

The Burgomeister got to his feet and squeezed the water from his sleeves.

"I'd suggest you toddle back over that bridge of yours," he quipped. "The Hellenburg Guard won't be happy if they find you moping around in their jurisdiction."

Dirk got to his feet and cursed the man under his breath.

There was nothing he could do.

He was out of options and out of luck.

The Burgomeister gave him a winning smile, bowed, then turned and started walking towards the woods behind him.

Dirk sighed.

He'd lost.

Everything he'd done had been for nothing.

"Sheenah," he whispered. "Why have you forsaken me...?"

Suddenly, Klept froze on the spot.

He gasped and his hands went up to his neck.

Dirk took a pace forward and noticed a thin line of cord wrapped around the man's neck.

Klept turned and beckoned Dirk to help him.

He tried to call out, but no sound left his mouth.

His face turned blue and he started to panic.

Dirk took another pace forward and then caught a glimpse of someone hiding within the treeline.

It was the assassin, Ertha Rouge.

She was holding onto the other end of the line, which had been thrown over the branch above.

Dirk reached for the dagger at his belt...

Then stayed his hand.

Klept gave him a look of desperation.

Dirk shook his head and removed his hand

from the hilt.

He let out a sigh then turned his back on the man, as Rouge began lifting him up off the ground.

As Dirk began walking back towards the bridge, his thoughts turned to the conversation he'd had with her outside Fryk's Casino.

He remembered berating her about her murder of Mollat, teasing her that she'd been sloppy and had left loose ends.

She promised him that in the future, she wouldn't.

It appeared to be a promise kept...

CHAPTER 16

Dirk gazed out of the Tavern window as a cold autumnal rain battered the streets of Flescher's Lane. Two weeks had passed since the Erntfest, and the long, glorious, summer of 1216 was finally over.

A change was in the air.

And it wasn't limited to the weather.

The events of that fateful day had changed Durnborg forever.

No longer was it a backwater provisional town in the Northern counties, but the epicentre of the revolutionary movement. For though the forces of the *Scarlet Faction* had been soundly defeated, and its leaders imprisoned on charges of sedition, news of their failed uprising had spread far across the land.

The apparatus of the Imperial machine could no longer ignore them.

The threat that they posed to the stability of the Empire was a real one, and the authorities were forced to conceded that what had happened in Durnborg was equally likely to happen elsewhere.

When Nye Yossell was hanged in the square a week after the coup, his execution was attended by a large number of people, most of whom turned out in red to show their support of a man they considered a martyr to their cause.

When the trapdoor of the gallows was opened, the crowd responded by raising their fists and bowing their heads.

It was a silent tribute, but it reverberated loudly.

"Why are you looking so glum?" Ing asked.

The Rhunligger was sitting across from him, with a tankard of ale in his hand.

"You do realise this is a party?"

Dirk smiled weakly.

He didn't feel in the mood to celebrate.

"A new Burgomeister won't solve this town's problems," Dirk remarked.

"No," Ing replied. "But aren't you happy that it's one of us in charge?"

Dirk glanced over to the bar, where a large crowd of well-wishers were gathered around Borton Hamm, the former Guildcaptain, who was now wearing the dark green robes of office. He looked happy and content, laughing and joking with them, as he sipped wine from his goblet.

Dirk knew it was nothing more than a mask.

Hamm no more wanted to be Burgomeister than Captain of the Guild.

Not that he'd had much choice in the matter.

The Emperor had sent a letter to Hamm, offering him the post. Dirk had heard that it had been written in such a way that compelled Hamm to accept, with the threat of ramifications if he did not.

It was an unusual move, for under the provisions of the *Finder's Covenant*, Guildsmen could not stand for office.

When some questioned its legality, the matter was swiftly tested in court, and Vor Ruis, the young Lawyer who had served as the Guild's Counsel at the Trial of Guildsergeant Bakker in Einhof, successfully argued in the Emperor's favour that since Hamm was *appointed*, and not *elected*, the decision should stand.

The citizens of Durnborg had rejoiced the verdict.

His theatrics at the *Erntfest* had become a popular figure, and the public had warmed to him for exposing the corruption in their midst. If he had stood for election under normal circumstances, there was no doubt he would have won.

"I just wish Klept could have faced justice," Dirk replied.

Ing laughed.

"I'm sure he will, one day," he said.

Dirk forced a smile.

"Maybe," he lied.

Following the events of the Erntfest, Dirk had told the Guild that Klept had escaped and was currently at large. He'd deliberately omitted any mention of Rouge, or what had really happened on the other side of the bridge.

It would have led to all sorts of questions being asked...

Questions he'd rather not answer.

He supped from his tankard and returned to the window.

The rain was getting heavier and in amongst the droplets he saw flakes of snow.

It was a sign that there would be a long, cold winter ahead.

Ing leaned forward to draw his attention.

"There's something I've been meaning to ask you," he said.

"What?" Dirk replied, as he watched a patrol of Guardsmen pass by, their green gambesons dusted with white powder.

Ing leant back in his seat.

"Why was Mollat so important to you?"

The question caught Dirk off-guard.

"What do you mean?" he asked.

"The man was a friendless miser," he explained. "He was loathed by everyone who knew him. Yet you went out of your way, risking your career, your reputation, even your life, to bring his killers to justice..."

Ing looked him in the eye.

"...Why?"

Dirk sighed.

"He reminded me of my father," he replied.

Ing looked at him, confused.

"How?" he asked.

"They were both murdered," Dirk replied. "And when they died, no one wanted to fight for them. Not even the Guild."

Ing smiled

"So, you wanted to set the record straight for Mollat?"

Dirk nodded.

Ing raised his glass.

"Then let us toast a job well done," he proposed.

Dirk smirked.

What he'd achieved had hardly been a victory.

"To the endless pursuit of Justice?" he countered.

Ing laughed.

"Go on, then," he chuckled. "But only because I'm thirsty."

Dirk shook his head, then raised his mug.

* * *

Hamm's party ran well into the night.

By the end, Ing was so drunk he couldn't walk.

"Take me back..." he slurred, as Dirk carried him out. "I need my bed.... And the privy."

He twisted himself under Dirk's arm then staggered through the snow to the nearest alleyway, where he opened his drawers and started pissing up the wall.

Dirk waited for him in the street, keeping an eye out for the guards.

Public urination was illegal in Durnborg, and it would not look good on Hamm's first day if his former charges were caught flouting the rules.

"Hurry up," Dirk said.

"I'm going as fast as I can," the Rhunligger replied, breezily.

A chill wind blew through streets.

Dirk shuddered and folded his arms over his chest.

The snow started to fall thicker now, with flakes the size of Two Dram bits.

Through the blizzard, he caught a glimpse of a figure coming towards him.

The man was hunched over, stumbling along as if he were drunk. He wore a dark coat whose tails fell below his knees.

He looked like a regular citizen, travelling home after a long night's drinking, but Dirk couldn't help but notice that there was something odd about him.

His movement seemed forced, as if his drunkenness was nothing but a pretence.

Dirk's hand drifted unconsciously to the hilt of his blade.

He watched the man suspiciously as he approached.

There was definitely something not right

here.

At once he wondered if the man had been sent by Ruul Zamar.

Had he been sent to call in his favour?

The man stumbled towards him.

Dirk stepped back against the wall.

The man glanced at him as he passed.

His eyes were glazed over, and stream of spittle dribbled from his mouth.

"G'evening," he slurred, as he staggered by.

Dirk exhaled a sigh of relief.

He was just a normal man.

Dirk watched as he continued up the road, brushing against the walls of the buildings as he wobbled home.

"What's happening?"

Ing's voice startled him.

He turned around to see his friend emerging from the alley, pulling up his breeches.

"Who was that?" he asked.

"No one," Dirk replied.

Ing sniffed.

"He looks like a drunk," he said, without a hint of irony.

He hiccupped loudly, then his face turned green.

"Come on," he said. "Let's get back... Before the Guard see us and think we're a couple of ne'er-do-wells..."

Dirk took his arm ad led him down the street to the Guildhouse. He opened the door and shunted his friend inside, then helped him up the stairs to his room.

Ing flopped down on his bed then buried his face in his pillow.

He began snoring almost immediately.

Dirk smiled and bade him goodnight.

Then he left the room and made his way down to corridor.

He felt tired now.

The day had been a long one and he wanted nothing more than to sleep.

As he arrived at his room, he was startled to find the door ajar.

A glow of candlelight shone through the crack.

Someone was inside his room.

His placed his hand on the hilt of his sword and pushed open the door.

Sitting on his bunk was Major Patz.

The man stood up when he entered and removed the smoking pipe from his lips.

"Guildsergeant," he said, acknowledging him.

"Patz," he replied. "What are you doing here?"

His hand immediately went to the hilt of his sword.

His former master-of-arms smiled.

"There's no need for that," he growled, blowing of plume of pungent smelling smoke into the air, "I come in peace."

"How can I believe that, after what you did to me in Einhof?"

Patz smirked.

"That was a personal matter," he said, "This is business."

Dirk laughed.

"Get out," he said. "Whatever it is you're selling, I'm not interested."

"Oh, I'm not here to sell you anything," the Major replied, with a twisted smile. "I came to deliver a message."

Dirk cut his eyes at the man.

"Whose message?" he asked.

"A mutual friend," Patz replied. "A certain Mr. Zamar of Kronnig."

Dirk suddenly remembered what had happened at the Mill, and what Ruul's goons had told him them his name was 'Mikken'.

"*Pull the other one*," they'd said. "*He only has one arm...*"

Dirk's eyes fixed on the fleshy stump protruding from the Major's right sleeve.

"You're the informer," he said. "You're Mikken."

Patz nodded and smiled.

"Clever boy," he replied. "Maybe you're not as 'unremarkable' as I once thought..."

During Bakker's trial, the Major had dismissed Dirk's aptitude to Guildsmanry, painting him as an average recruit with no exceptional talents.

The sleight had stuck in Dirk's craw.

"Enough of this," he hissed. "Ruul's message.

What is it?"

The Major smirked.

"You're to go to Hessell," he began. "To Wernerliecht, the Capital. There you will meet a man by the name of Yuvroum, at the Kingfisher Tavern, who'll give you further instructions."

"Who is this Yuvroum?" Dirk asked.

"He's Ruul's man in Hessell," the Major replied.

"And how am I to get there?"

Patz put down his pipe, slid his hand beneath the lapel of his tunic, and pulled out an envelope.

"A month's leave of absence," he said, handing it to Dirk. "Signed by Guildmaster Patrick, and a ticket to board *The Emperor's Fury.* It sets sail from Kronnig tomorrow night. Make sure you're on board."

Dirk opened seal and removed the letters.

"And what if I'm not?" he asked.

Patz smirked.

"Then you'll be dead by the following morn."

Dirk studied the papers in his hand.

"I'd feel a lot happier about this if I knew what I was letting in for," he remarked.

The Major sighed.

"You get used to it...." he replied, ruefully.

APPENDICES

Geography

Ethren – A Realm of Kingdoms located to the North West of the Great Continent, consisting of the Gerwaldian Empire and the Kingdoms of Westren. The common language is *Prutch*.

Western Ocean – A large ocean lying off the western cost of Westren.

Middle Sea – A small sea that separates Grexia from the continent of Kulaani.

Gerwald – Kingdom in Eastern Ethren
    Royal Kronnig – Capital City of the Empire of Gerwald, located centrally on the River Rhund.
    Hellenburg – A City in central Gerwald.
    Einhof – A town in eastern Gerwald, headquarters of the Guild Corps.
    Durnborg – A small town in northern Gerwald.
    Berghof - A small village, north of Durnborg.
    Rhund – A town in Gerwald.
    Bruun - A village in Gerwald.

Brynnig - A town in Gerwald

The River Rhund – A major waterway that flows from the Grondils through the Gerwaldian Empire and Gefghed to the Middle Sea.

The River Wynt - A tributary of the River Rhund.

The River Wyl - A tributary of the River Rhund

Westren – The collective name for the Kingdoms of Hussfalt, Hessell, La Broque and Grexia.

Hessell – Western Ethren Kingdom, located south of the River Soude and north of the River Slou, bordered by the Grondil Mountains to the East.

Wernerliecht – Capital of Hessell, which sits at the mouth of the River Slou.

Eindbosch – A town in southeast Hessell, sitting in the foothills of the Grondil Range.

The Rivertowns – Collective name for Grente, Grice and Utterdam: the three major towns that are situated on the River Soude.

Grente – Port city to the North West of Hessell. Famous for its bridge, named after the Hessellian Prince Wendell, and University.

Grente Quarry – A prison and quarry that is famous for its sandstone.

Leiderbrugge – a small town within the county of Grente.

Woergeld – a small town within the county of Grente.

Utterdam – A city on the banks of the Soude, lying East of the town of Grice. Houses the Guildschool of Hessell and Utterdam Sanctuary.

Grice – A town on the banks of the Soude, lying to the West of Utterdam.

Delstad – A small village in Western Hessell, most famous for the Delstad Estate, a vast stately built upon the coastal cliffs.

The River Slou – A border river that divides the Kingdoms of Hessell and La Broque

The Soude – A border river that divides the kingdoms of Hessell and Hussfalt.

> **The Northern Byway** – The main road connecting the three Rivertowns.

Grondil – A mountainous region in the northwest of Hessell, also the source of the River Soude.

> **Siegmur's Pass** – A pass in the Grondil range that links the Kingdoms of Hussfalt and Hessell, now closed following a rock fall.

> **Baan** – A large village in the Grondil foothills, famous for its timber products.

Hussfalt – A Westren Kingdom, located to the immediate north of the River Soude

Busque – Capital City of Hussfalt.

Marnberg – a small village that sits near the Striffen Line.

Bladenhaal – A village in Hussfalt, the site of a famous battle.

Kronnick – A town in Hussfalt, site of a famous battle during the Great Westren War.

Wemmelford – A village in Hussfalt.

Deneul – River in southern Hussfalt.

Thishen – A village in eastern Hussfalt.

Striffen Line - A heavily fortified range of hills roughly five miles to the north of Grice.

La Broque – A Westren Kingdom located to the South of Hessell.

Slou – A river in that marks the border between La Broque and Hessell.

Pendforte – a city in the Kingdom of La Broque, South West of Ethren.

Basteaux – A village in the Kingdom of La Broque, South West of Ethren.

Grexia – Kingdom in South Westren, said to be the oldest Kingdom in Ethren.

Corinthe – Capital of Grexia.

Summer Festival – An annual event featuring the best travelling circuses in all of Ethren.

Temple of the Saints – A famous cathedral, and permanent residence of the Grand Alterman, spiritual leader of the

V'Loirean faith.

Doran – A small village in eastern Grexia that sits on the coast of the Middle Sea.

Nysos – A port town in eastern Grexia that sits on the coast of the Middle Sea.

Daxus – An island city-state, aligned to the Kingdom of Grexia.

Harardren – A Kingdom in the Northern Realms. It is located North of Hussfalt, beyond the River Vardeaen and is chiefly populated by Dwarfs.

> **River Vardeaen** – River that separates Westren from the Northern Realms.
>
> **Bim-Lodhar** – Capital of Harardren.
>
> **Heg-Logar** - City located in Harardren, famous for the *Grey Kirk*, a famous V'Loirean Cathedral.

Kulaani – A Realm of Kingdoms located to the south of the Gerwaldian colonies of Tibrut and Marmur.

> **B'Naatu** – A city in Kulaani, south of the Gerwaldian colonies of Tibrut and Marmur.

Gefghed – A kingdom located to the south east of Ethren, currently under the rule of the Gerwaldian Empire. It is sometimes known as *Shemali*.

> **Ghis** – Capital of Gefghed, located in the West of the Kingdom, at the mouth of the River Rhund.
>
> **Shemali** – A small town on the River Rhund.
>
> **Shafarr** – A small village lying on the edge of

Shula's Gorge.

Shida – A small village in Gefghed and rumoured birthplace of the prophet V'Loire.

The Silent Valley –A dry canyon that marks the border between Gerwald and Gefghed.

Veleenum – The last Kingdom of the Elves, located to the East of Gerwald in the Zamur Mountains.

Characters

Guildsmen
Dirk Vanslow – A Guildsman.

Ing Rhunlig - A Guildsman, serving in Durnborg.

Guildcaptain Borton Hamm - Commanding Officer of the Guild of Finders in Durnborg

Errol - Clerk of the Durnborg Guild

Hogar - A Guildsman, serving in Durnborg.

Vargas - Guildsergeant of the Guild of Finders in Durnborg

Guildmaster Patrick – Head of the Gerwaldian Guildschool in Royal Kronnig.

Major Patz – Master of Arms at the Gerwaldian Guildschool in Royal Kronnig.

Coen – A Guildsman.

Ing – A Guildsman.

Grulsch - a Guildsman

Guildsergeant Bakker – Leader of the Red Vipers of Ghis.

Varek – A Guildsman serving with the Red Vipers.

Mu'Ungo – A Kulaanian Guildsman serving with the Red Vipers.

Ermus – A Guildsman serving with the Red Vipers.

Kort – A Grexian Guildsman serving with the Red Vipers.

Boors – A Half-Dwarf Guildsman serving with the Red Vipers.

Citizens of Ghis

Minas Vanslow – Father of Dirk Vanslow.

Ruyven – a former Rebel, now owner of Ruyven's Rums.

Rebels

Araxys Delefries - Rebel leader of the Swords of Sheenah.

Marfine Delefries - A rebel, serving with Swords of Sheenah, daughter of Araxys.

Olojeon Hax – A rebel, serving with Swords of Sheenah.

Tressyn – A rebel, serving with Swords of Sheenah.

Dustyn – A rebel, serving with Swords of Sheenah.

Einhof

Justice Arneld – A Magistrate

Vor Ruis – A young lawyer

Durnborg

Burgomeister Kohn Klept – Burgomeister (Mayor) of Durnborg

Kurgen Mollat - a rich, miserly landowner

Ruystin Fryk - a Bookkeeper.

Klug - A Ogre. Ruystin Fryk's bodyguard.

Nye Yossel - a petty criminal

Armil Grynn - Head of the Agricultural Union.

Ralph Olberwalt - A champion prize-fighter.

Royal Kronnig

Ruul Zamar - Leader of the Night Owls, the largest criminal gang in Gerwald

Ertha Rouge – An assassin, who works for Ruul Zamar.

Bartheld – Innkeep and owner of the Emperor's Legs.

Rangill Jurghoof - A merchant.

Religion & Tradition

Religion
V'Loire – God-Prophet and founder of the V'Loirean Faith.

The Testament – The holy book of the V'Loirean Faith

St. Felix – One of V'Loire's nine disciples, known as *The Beastmaster* or *Master of Beasts*.

St. Greta – One of V'Loire's nine disciples, known as the *Prophet of Doom*, as it was said she could foresee the future.

St. Unglebus – One of V'Loire's nine disciples, a patron of the arts, who came to be known as *The Drinker*.

St. Rinda - One of V'Loire's nine disciples, a patron of the sciences, who came to be known as *The Philosopher*.

Sheenah – God-Prophet and founder of the Sheenahic Faith.

The She'En – The holy book of the Sheenahic Faith.

Tekat – A god of death, whose worshippers make human sacrifices. Also known as the *Horned God* or the *Horned Devil*.

Tradition
Gerwald
The Erntfest - Festival of Harvest, which

takes place at the end of Vierjar, the fourth month of the Gerwaldian Calendar.

Politics & History

Gerwald

Government - Imperial Monarchy. Founded after the *War of Ascension* in 1143. The Head of State is Emperor Tomas II.

The Guild

The Hunter's Purge - An event that took place in 1162, following the kidnapping of Prince Alfons of La Broque, which preceded the signing of *The Finder's Covenant*, an agreement which granted the Guild exclusive rights to all new warrants issued in Gerwald and the Kingdoms of Westren.

Printed in Great Britain
by Amazon